Spells and Spiced Latte – A Coffee
Witch Cozy Mystery – Maddie Goodwell
1

By

Jinty James

CHAPTER 1

"I'll have my usual, Maddie." A woman in her early fifties with wavy light brown hair and a trim figure stepped up to the counter of the coffee truck.

"One spiced latte coming up, Joan." Maddie Goodwell smiled at one of her regular customers, then began steaming milk.

Ever since she'd started her own coffee truck, Brewed from the Bean, parked at the square in Estherville, a small town one hundred miles from Seattle, business had been brisk. — brisk :

Painted brown coffee beans danced on the outside of the truck, while inside, the décor was a calming cream, with a professional coffee machine grinding and hissing most of the day.

Large piles of to-go cups in small, regular, and large sizes were stacked on one side of the machine, ready for the next coffee she made.

Maddie had quit her job at the local café six months ago. She couldn't bear to

(everybody loves coffee

1

work for Claudine, the mean-spirited and curmudgeonly new owner.

At first, she'd been dubious about her friend Suzanne's suggestion – best friends since middle school – that they start their own coffee truck business, but when Suzanne's brother found them a cheap food truck that he helped them remodel inexpensively, she and Suzanne pooled their remaining savings to invest in the best coffee machine they could afford. After that, they were in business. And it had been good from the start.

"We should start making our own cookies," Suzanne's voice broke into her thoughts. "We could make a lot of extra money."

"You're right." Maddie pulled the shot of coffee, adding the steaming milk until it looked as tempting as she could make it. "We'll talk about it after the morning rush."

"Great." Suzanne grinned, her strawberry blonde hair swinging from side to side in a neat ponytail, her bangs framing her wholesome face. Her blue eyes and snub nose dusted with freckles

2

gave her a look that was wholesome with
a side of slightly sexy.

Maddie was just about to hand over the
coffee when she hesitated. Her customer
Joan was usually cheerful, but today she
seemed a little down. Surely it wouldn't
hurt if she peeked into Joan's future for
the next twenty-four hours?

"Show me," Maddie whispered,
brushing back her brown hair as she stared
at the top layer of foam on the latte. The
foam swirled, then cleared. The woman
standing in front of her, waiting
expectantly for her coffee, lay dead on a
kitchen floor.

Maddie froze. Whatever she had
expected to see, it hadn't been *that*.

"Maddie, are you okay?" Suzanne
asked, touching her arm.

Maddie blinked, as if by doing so, she
could make the last minute never happen.

"Yeah." She cleared her throat.
Handing the spiced latte to Joan, she said,
"You must be very careful over the next
couple of days."

Joan looked puzzled as she took the
paper cup. "I usually am." She forced a

Handwritten margin notes:
what does looking into one's
future do? it's going to happen
regardless,
right?
won't it
hurt more
knowing
what is to
happen but
not being
able to
help and
change it!
or is that
just her
future
now?
is it
uncertain?

(girl, i would
be her
body guard
today.

3

laugh. "In fact, my husband keeps telling me how boring I am."

How could Maddie tell her customer what she just saw in the coffee foam? For the last twenty years, ever since she'd been seven years old, she'd been able to foretell someone's future for the next twenty-four hours on the surface of a freshly made coffee. Only in coffee. It didn't happen any other way. She had never seen someone's murder before!

"I mean it," Maddie insisted, not wanting to freak out the older woman, but wanting her to take the warning seriously. "Be very careful."

"I will," Joan replied, picking up her coffee and taking a sip. "Mmm, just as good as usual, Maddie. I love the cinnamon in it. You really have a knack."

"Thanks." Maddie's smile was strained as she watched Joan turn and head toward across the town square. Another customer stepped up to the counter, demanding Maddie's attention, as Joan walked out of sight.

***

4

At seven, Maddie, who haunted the local used bookshop, stumbled across a thick, old book called *Wytchcraft for the Chosen*. She paid the one dollar the bookshop owner insisted was the price just for her, and sneaked it home, certain her conservative parents would not approve.

Her mother was a high school teacher and her dad was an accountant. Mom helped out with the PTA, and Dad helped her with her math homework. She thought they probably hadn't even tried to do a real magic spell in their lives.

At night, she read the book by torchlight, thrilling at the yellow spotted pages and old-fashioned words, some she had to sound out in a whisper.

One spell in particular caught her attention – how to tell someone's future for the next twenty-four hours with the aid of a cup of coffee.

She'd gotten up early the next morning, tiptoeing into the kitchen, and made a mug of instant coffee, hoping her parents didn't hear her.

When brewing finished, she stared into the dark depths, silently saying the words of the spell – the book had made it plain that no one was to hear the actual words of the incantation, or it wouldn't work – apart from the last two words – *Show me*.

"Show me," seven-year-old Maddie had whispered.

The surface of the coffee swirled, then cleared, showing an image of herself playing on the swing set at school.

She'd been excited – and scared – that the spell had worked. And later that day, she'd been playing on the swing set at school, just like the vision had shown her!

But that had been the only spell she had ever been able to cast. She'd attempted lots of others from the book, and none of them had been successful.

Over and over, Maddie tried the coffee invocation, and each time it worked. But if she made the coffee for herself – not that she enjoyed the taste of it at age seven – she only saw a glimpse of her future for the next twenty-four hours. Nobody else's.

When she'd started working at the coffee shop after college, not sure what she wanted to do career wise, whenever a whisper of intuition nudged her to do so, she peeked into her customer's future. And in each case, it worked. Usually she saw pleasant images, like a woman being proposed to in a fancy restaurant, or a man getting the raise he desperately needed.

But she had never seen a crime before.

***

"Phew!" Suzanne flopped onto a stool inside the coffee truck. "That morning rush was insane!"

"I know," Maddie agreed, sitting on the stool opposite.

"Mrrow." Trixie the cat eyed the two of them as if in agreement. A large white Persian, she had glowing turquoise eyes and a silver spine and tail. Everyone remarked on her unusual coloring, but Maddie always wondered if the reason was because Trixie wasn't a normal cat.

Was she a witch's familiar?

Her familiar?

Somehow, nobody had batted an eye at the Persian appearing in the coffee truck from time to time. Not even the health inspector, after Maddie had first opened for business. Was it possible that Trixie had something to do with that?

7

One year ago, when Maddie had turned twenty-six, Trixie had wandered into the coffee shop where Maddie had worked. She'd sat on the floor beneath the counter, looking up at Maddie.

"Mrrow," the cat had greeted Maddie.

"Are you lost?" Maddie stepped from around the coffee machine and bent down.

"Mrrow."

She could have sworn that sound had sounded like "No."

Claudine, the new owner, came out from the back and had started shouting at the cat, telling it to get out or else!

Instinctively, Maddie scooped up the feline and hurried outside, turning back to scowl at her boss, before carrying the pretty cat home.

"You can stay with me until I find your owner," Maddie had whispered to the Persian, the soft white fur tickling her fingers. The cat nestled in her arms, as if there was nowhere else she'd rather be.

As Maddie hurried back to work, she shook off the ridiculous thought that the Persian had been trying to tell her that she belonged to Maddie.

But still …

Her mind flashed back to the ancient tome on witchcraft she'd bought when she was seven. Towards the back of the book, a crumbling page had stated that a true witch didn't come into her full powers until she turned seven-and-twenty.

"I'm only twenty-six," she reassured herself. Why would a witch's familiar arrive now, when the only spell she could do was to foretell people's future for the next twenty-four hours in a cup of coffee? It didn't make sense.

But the thought stayed in her mind for the rest of the day and during her birthday dinner.

When she arrived home, the cat was still there, curled up asleep on the sofa, her head nestled against a cushion, as if she'd lived there all her life.

The next day Maddie had visited the local vet, and the sheriff's department. But nobody had reported a missing white Persian cat. She'd scoured the local newspaper, but there weren't any ads about lost pets.

She gave her details to the vet, just in case someone did report losing their cat, but she never heard back from them.

It looked like the feline had chosen to live with her.

A couple of days later, when she'd been looking through the book on witchcraft, the Persian had sat next to her, staring at each page, as if she could actually read the ancient words.

"What should I call you?" Maddie asked softly.

"Triii…"

The cat trilled, the first-time Maddie had heard her do so.

She furrowed her brow, glancing from the gorgeous cat to the old book and back again.

"Trixie," she said slowly, somehow feeling that was the perfect name to call her.

"Mrrow." The cat closed her eyes and rubbed her face against Maddie's arm.

"Trixie the cat." A smile tilted Maddie's lips.

***

"Hey, are you okay?" Suzanne looked at Maddie in concern as they recovered from the morning rush. "You didn't look very well after you made Joan her latte."

Maddie hesitated. Her friend knew about her ability to cast the coffee vision spell, and had believed her when she haltingly confided in her a year ago that she thought Trixie might be her familiar, even though she had a year to go until she received her full witchy powers.

In fact, she'd told Suzanne about *Wytchraft for the Chosen* years ago.

But should she tell her friend what she'd just seen?

Trixie the cat nudged her arm, as if encouraging her to confide in Suzanne.

"I saw Joan lying dead in a kitchen," Maddie blurted out.

"What?" Suzanne's eyes widened. "Are you sure?"

"Positive." Maddie nodded.

"What are you going to do?" Suzanne asked.

"Do?"

"Did you warn Joan?"

"Yes," Maddie replied. "But how could I tell her I saw a vision of her lying dead? And," she hesitated, "it looked like her head was bloody."

11

"You mean, murdered?" Suzanne's hand flew to her mouth.

"I don't know. Maybe she tripped and hit her head and that's why it looked like blood."

"Are you going to tell the sheriff's department?" Suzanne asked.

"And say, 'Hi guys, I'm a witch, and by the way, I cast a spell on Joan's coffee this morning and saw her lying dead on the floor.'" Maddie shook her head. "Do you think they – or anyone else – would believe me?"

"I believe you," Suzanne said loyally.

"I know." Maddie allowed herself to smile. "And you have no idea how grateful I've been that you believed me when I told you about what I could do."

"They'd probably laugh me out of the station," Maddie added, frowning.

"Then they're idiots," Suzanne said fiercely. "These days, with all the TV shows about witches and mediums, as well as some police departments using clairvoyants to help solve cases, you'd think they'd have an open mind."

"I know." Maddie sighed. "But you're the only one I've told about the witchcraft book—" she glanced at her cat, "—apart from Trixie. Whenever I look through the book, she's right by my side, practically turning the pages with me."

"Perhaps she's encouraging you to try some different spells."

"None of the others have worked." Maddie shrugged. "Even though I've just turned twenty-seven – or seven-and-twenty as written in the book – nothing happens. The only spell I can do is the coffee vision spell."

"Maybe you need to wait for the next full moon." Suzanne snapped her fingers. "Maybe they counted time a little differently back then – you said yourself the book looks like it's a few hundred years old."

smart

Maddie nodded.

"So maybe according to the book, you're not twenty-seven yet. Maybe next month any spell you try will work."

"Or maybe none of them will," Maddie countered, stroking Trixie. The cat purred, closing her eyes to little turquoise slits.

"I bet I'm right," Suzanne insisted. "Anyone looking at you and Trixie can tell you're meant to be together."

"Do you think so?" Pleasure flickered through Maddie. "I can't believe I've only had her a year – or maybe she's had me." She smiled. "It's hard to remember what my life was like without her."

Suzanne nodded. "All the more reason that my theory is correct. You *are* a real witch, and Trixie is your familiar."

"Mrrow," Trixie said, as if in agreement.

CHAPTER 2

"But what are we going to do about Joan?" Suzanne asked, drinking from the bottled water she carried around with her everywhere.

"I don't know," Maddie admitted. "I don't know anything about her, apart from the fact she comes here for coffee a few times per week."

"I think her husband is the head librarian," Suzanne said thoughtfully, tapping the plastic water bottle against her lips. "I was at the library one day browsing through the new books, and I saw her talking to him, as if they knew each other."

"I haven't been to the library for a while," Maddie said ruefully. "I've been too busy." She glanced around at the interior of the food truck.

"I know what you mean," Suzanne replied. "I've only managed to read one of those new books I borrowed, and then I forgot to take them all back and had to pay overdue fines."

Both of them giggled, then quickly sobered.

"Do you think I should warn Joan again?" Maddie asked.

"We could go after work," Suzanne agreed, before moving to the counter to greet a customer.

***

Maddie, Trixie, and Suzanne closed down the food truck at four o'clock. They'd experimented closing at different hours in the past and tallying the daily sales, finally agreeing that shutting down at 4 p.m. seemed to be the sweet spot. It was late enough that they didn't miss many customers, but early enough to still get some personal things done if they needed to, or have time to just hang out together without the pressure of making what seemed like hundreds of coffees each day.

"Come on," Maddie said, starting up the food truck and heading toward her house. Part of the town's rules was that she could park her truck in the town square since she was offering a service to

16

the residents, as long as she was quiet and respectful, but she couldn't leave the truck there overnight. So even though she only lived a two-minute walk away from the square, she had to drive the truck home every afternoon.

"We can take my car to Joan's house and warn her," Maddie continued as she parked outside her cottage.

"Mrrow?" Trixie inquired.

"Maybe you should stay at home, Trix," Maddie told her.

"Broomf!" Trixie's face scrunched up.

"Did Trixie just blow a raspberry at you?" Suzanne struggled to contain a grin.

"It's not the first time." Maddie rolled her eyes. "But she's been in the food truck all day – I thought she'd like to have some time to herself or go play in the garden."

Trixie's tail swished and her eyes narrowed.

"I don't think that's what she wants to do," Suzanne pointed out.

"Fine." Maddie sighed. "You can come with us, Trixie." To Suzanne she added, "You have no idea how she bosses me around at times."

"I can imagine," Suzanne said drily.

17

Maddie got out of the truck and picked up the Persian. "We're going in my car, Trix."

A loud raspy purr escaped from the feline's throat and she snuggled her face against Maddie's chest, as if in approval.

Suzanne's faint laughter followed them as they got into Maddie's white compact car.

"Do you know where Joan lives?" Maddie asked as she turned on the ignition. Suzanne sat in the front, holding Trixie.

"Mom and Dad went to a party they held at their house years ago. I think it was on Pine Lane. I remember Mom saying the house had an unusual turret at the top."

"I know where that street is." Maddie reversed out of the driveway and turned right, away from the town square.

A few minutes later, she pulled up outside a tan brick house, a small turret with cream shutters jutting out at the top of the dwelling.

"Yes, this must be it," Suzanne said, pointing out the name *Hodgeton* painted on the large mailbox.

Trixie the cat had her nose pressed to the side window, her ears pricked in anticipation.

Did her cat really know what they were doing? It wasn't the first time Maddie had asked herself that question. At times, her fluffy white Persian seemed almost human, as if she could totally understand everything Maddie told her. But at other times, it was as if Trixie couldn't understand a word – or maybe that was what she wanted Maddie to believe, so she could get her own way. Maddie loved Trixie dearly, but she could be a handful at times.

"Trixie, you'll have to stay in the car," Maddie said firmly as she got out and swiftly shut the door.

"You heard Maddie." Suzanne gently placed the cat in the driver's seat, slid out, and closed the door.

Trixie swished her tail and turned her back to them, before curling up in the car seat and closing her eyes, as if the two of them didn't exist.

"I think Trixie's cross with us," Suzanne said as they started up the path to the house. Plain green lawn greeted them on either side of the path, and a big red rose bush with flowers in full bloom dominated one corner of the garden.

"Yeah." Maddie sighed.

They rang the brass doorbell which seemed in keeping with the turret above them.

Ding dong.

Silence.

Maddie and Suzanne looked at each other.

"I'll press it again." Maddie pushed the button once more.

Ding dong.

Silence.

"I don't think anyone's home," Suzanne said.

"Yeah." Maddie frowned. "There isn't a car in the driveway, but that doesn't mean anything. It might be in the garage."

Suzanne looked at her watch. "The library will be closed by now, so I don't think Joan will be there."

"I don't want to wait for her husband to come home." Maddie hesitated. "What if he's involved somehow – if the vision is true?"

"No way!" Suzanne shook her head. "When I saw them talking at the library that day, they just seemed like an ordinary couple – I didn't get any kind of weird vibe from them."

"That's good to know." Relief flickered through Maddie. "But still …"

"I get it." Suzanne touched her friend's arm. "But just because you saw her … dead … doesn't mean it will actually happen, does it? I mean, haven't you had a vision before that didn't come true?"

"That's right." Maddie nodded. "A few of them over the years, and it's not like I cast the coffee spell every day – well, not before I started working as a barista, anyway. The only explanation I've come up with is that what I see in the coffee cup is only a possibility that can happen in the next twenty-four hours – it's not set in stone."

"So maybe nothing will happen to Joan and she'll be at the truck tomorrow ordering a latte," Suzanne said, looking relieved.

"I certainly hope so."

***

Maddie spent the night tossing and turning, disturbing Trixie, who slept on the other side of the double bed. But she couldn't shake off the feeling that the vision might come true.

Who would want to kill Joan? Why?

She and Suzanne had stayed at Joan's house for about twenty minutes, alternately ringing the bell and waiting – hoping – for someone to answer the door, until they decided Joan wasn't home. And for the reasons she'd stated to Suzanne, Maddie was reluctant to wait until Joan's husband returned home from work.

If only Joan had been there! She would have cautioned the older woman once more to be careful. But would Joan have heeded the warning? Or would she think Maddie was weird? But how could she tell Joan the truth – that she thought she was a witch, albeit one who could only cast one spell correctly – and that she had seen a vision of Joan's death. No one knew the truth apart from Suzanne and Trixie the cat.

When the alarm buzzed at 6.30 a.m., Maddie was already wide awake.

"Broomf!" Trixie ignored the buzzing and curled up in a tighter ball, her silver tail firmly wrapped around her furry body.

Usually the Persian pounced on her to get up just before the alarm sounded. Maybe Maddie's restless night had truly disturbed the cat.

Maddie grabbed a quick shower, spooned some of Trixie's favorite cat food into her turquoise bowl, then poured herself a bowl of cereal.

She glanced at the white and silver kitchen clock. Almost time to drive the coffee truck to the town square for the early morning joggers. In addition to coffee, she also sold hot tea and bottled water, both of which joggers seemed to enjoy, especially those exercising to lose weight.

Maddie entered the bedroom and grabbed her purse.

"I'm going to work, Trix," she spoke softly to the snoozing feline. "Do you want to stay here today?"

"Broomf." The cat snuggled deeper into the pastel blue and lilac patchwork quilt on top of the bed.

Maddie took that as a yes.

"Is Trixie still mad at you?" Suzanne asked as she hopped up into the food truck. Their official opening time was 7.30 a.m. but if they were ready a few minutes earlier, that's when they started serving customers.

"Yes." Maddie grimaced. "Or else she's tired from all my tossing and turning last night – heck, I'm exhausted from it!"

She turned to smile at a sweaty jogger, his middle-aged bald head gleaming with perspiration – as well as the rest of him.

"Water," he gasped, "please."

Maddie handed him a bottle of chilled water, taking the slightly damp bills from his hand and giving him the change.

"Thanks." He tore off the cap and chugged the contents of the bottle. "Thanks," he said again in a more normal voice, before half-walking, half-jogging away.

"It was a genius idea of yours to sell water as well," Maddie said. "I can't believe how many joggers don't carry a small bottle with them."

24

"I know." Suzanne nodded. "And I was thinking, what if we start making those health balls that you see everywhere? You know, the ones with "cacao—"" she made fingers quotes in the air, "—and coconut, dates, and all that disgustingly healthy stuff." She snapped her fingers. "Maybe we could add coffee to give them a boost!"

"It's a good idea." Maddie nodded. "But when are we going to find time to make them? After work?"

Suzanne eyed the interior of the truck. "I could make them during our non-busy times. It's all raw ingredients, so I don't need to bake anything. And it will be okay to make them in the truck because of your permit. All I'll need is a food processor."

"I've got one at home." Maddie's eyes lit up. "Why don't we find a recipe and buy the ingredients this afternoon? We could start making them tomorrow morning."

"Already got a recipe." Suzanne waved her phone in the air. "I did an online search last night. You know how I was talking yesterday about how we should make cookies or something to improve our profit margin? Well, I think these health balls will work out even better, since we don't have to bake them. And I bet the joggers will buy them, whereas they probably wouldn't buy cookies, as they'd feel guilty."

"Awesome!" They high-fived each other.

Another sweaty jogger stumbled to the counter, and they turned their attention to their new customer, the first of many for the following hour.

During the morning rush period, Maddie scanned the customers lining up for coffee, tea, or bottled water, but she couldn't see Joan anywhere.

She gnawed her lower lip. Suzanne's idea about making health balls had helped take her mind off the vision she'd seen yesterday, but now her anxiety returned full force.

It wasn't as if Joan had regular days that she visited the coffee truck. Maddie tried to think which mornings Joan had ordered a beverage last week, but couldn't quite remember. The older woman was only one of many regular customers she had. Although Maddie knew her regulars by sight, she was so slammed during the busy times that she focused solely on making the best drink she could each time, and not the exact time each customer arrived.

Was Joan okay? She only hoped the vision hadn't come true.

Towards the end of their busy morning, a woman with red-rimmed eyes walked up to the counter. She held a crumpled tissue to her nose, and her short dark hair looked messy, as if she'd torn her fingers through it.

"Just give me a black coffee. Please." She blew her nose.

"Are you all right?" Maddie asked, foreboding chilling her veins. She couldn't remember this customer before, but something about her set warning bells clanging in her mind.

"No." The woman sniffed. "And I feel so guilty ordering a coffee right now, but I don't know what to do with myself. My best friend Joan has been murdered!"

CHAPTER 3

"What?" Maddie gasped.

The woman nodded. "A detective has just finished talking to me. They wanted to know if I heard or saw something."

"Did you?" Maddie asked.

"No." The woman shook her head, regret chasing her features. "I wasn't home."

Maddie was so transfixed by the terrible news that her vision had come true, that she didn't notice Suzanne subtly nudging her out of the way and beginning to make a black coffee for the customer.

"Do you know how…" Maddie swallowed, "… Joan died?"

The woman nodded, tears beginning to stream down her face again.

"They said she was hit over the head with a crystal vase." She sniffed. "Joan loved that vase. And apparently, it held red roses from her garden in it. How could anyone do such a thing?" The woman blew into a sodden tissue.

"Where was she found?" Maddie asked, trying to be delicate.

"In her kitchen," the woman gulped.

Just like her vision - apart from the fact that a vase hadn't featured in the image that had arisen in the coffee cup yesterday.

"Here you go." Suzanne handed a steaming paper cup to the distraught woman. "On the house."

"Oh," the woman swallowed, as if trying to find her voice. "Thank you, girls. That's very kind."

"Do they know when she was … killed?" Suzanne asked.

"This morning!" The woman turned around, as if expecting to see a potential murderer standing right behind her, but only a puzzled looking senior citizen with tightly permed gray hair waited in line. "Her husband found her!"

Maddie frowned. "Does he work at the library?"

"That's right. He's the head librarian." The woman shook her head. "They've been married for so long – even longer than myself and my husband." She heaved a sigh. "I just don't know how he's taking the news. I wanted to go over there and see how he was, but the detective wouldn't let me." She sniffed. "They said they were just doing their job, and needed to speak to him right away."

"I'm so sorry," Maddie said, guilt running through her. She hadn't been able to warn Joan in time! She didn't know if that would have made a difference or not, but what was the point of having the power to cast such a spell if something terrible like this happened and she had no way to stop it?

"Thank you, dear." The woman took a sip from the cup. "Joan kept telling me how delicious your coffee was, but I'm not a big coffee drinker. This is very good, though."

"Thank you." Maddie forced her lips to move upwards in a semblance of a smile.

The woman nodded, then left, allowing the gray-haired senior citizen behind her to place her order.

Maddie numbly set about making a cappuccino on auto-pilot.

She shouldn't have left Joan's house until she'd spoken to her last night and warned her about the vision she'd seen. Joan might still be alive if she'd done so. Instead, Maddie had taken the easy way out and gone home.

For the next couple of hours, half of her customers seemed to have heard about Joan's murder and muttered about it among themselves. One old man with a bundle of library books under his arm even complained about the library not being open when he'd turned up on the dot of nine o'clock. Apparently, Joan's husband, being the head librarian, was in charge of opening the library in the mornings and closing up at night.

"Now my books are going to be overdue," the grizzled old man grumbled, before picking up his coffee and taking a little sip before walking off.

When there wasn't another customer in sight, Suzanne looked at Maddie. "Do you want to close up for the day?"

"Because it's my fault Joan was killed?" Maddie shook her head.

"It wasn't your fault," Suzanne said loyally. "You didn't kill her."

"But I didn't tell her what I saw in my vision." Maddie slammed a stack of paper cups onto the counter. "I didn't hang around her house until she came back so I could warn her properly."

31

"Even if you had, it doesn't mean she wouldn't have been murdered," Suzanne pointed out. "The killer didn't know about you having a vision. If he – or she – did, then maybe they would have had second thoughts."

A sudden thought struck Maddie, chilling her veins.

"Suzanne, don't tell anyone about my vision. What if word gets out and the killer think I know who did it?"

"You might be next." Suzanne paled.

Maddie swallowed hard. "If anything does happen to me, promise you'll look after Trixie."

"You know I will." Suzanne nodded.

"Unless …" Maddie hesitated, "… unless she finds another witch to live with. I often wonder how she just turned up like that, at the coffee shop, and why nobody reported a lost cat."

"Don't worry." Suzanne patted her arm. "If Trixie wants to live with me, I'll take good care of her. And if she wants to live with another—" she lowered her voice "—witch, I'll make sure she's happy there."

"Thanks." Maddie hugged her friend, blinking back sudden tears.

"But this isn't going to happen," Suzanne injected a bright note into her voice. "Because no one will find out about what you saw."

"I hope not." Maddie stiffened her spine. "Because we've got a lot to do. Since I feel it's my fault Joan was murdered, I'm going to find out who did it."

CHAPTER 4

"How are you going to do that?" Suzanne asked.

"Any way I can," Maddie said determinedly. "For instance – oh, it's Joan's neighbor, who ordered a black coffee a couple of hours ago. Mind the truck!" She dashed off across the green square, dodging a young woman wheeling a pram along the concrete path that bisected the expanse of green lawn.

Maddie puffed, out of breath, as she caught up with their customer outside a boutique, the warmth of the Spring sun shining down on them.

"Hi," she tried to catch her breath, hoping her face didn't look as red as it felt. She really must get more exercise – after she discovered who the killer was.

"Hi." The woman's eyes now looked pink around the rims instead of red raw. She summoned a smile. "Thank you again for the coffee." Blinking, she set her lips in a firm line. "I've told myself not to cry any more today."

"I think it's okay if you do," Maddie said gently, feeling like a heel for her ulterior motive in hailing the woman. "I just can't believe someone killed Joan," she continued, each word the absolute truth.

"I know!" The woman burst out. "If only I hadn't cancelled jogging with her this morning. But I wasn't feeling well—" she dropped her gaze "—and now I feel terrible. Because if we'd been out jogging, maybe she wouldn't have been murdered."

The woman sniffed, her eyes blinking.

"Oh, I'm sorry," Maddie said sincerely.

"I'm Linda, by the way." She dug out a clean tissue from her purse and wiped her eyes. "I've lived next to Joan for the last fifteen years. We were more than just neighbors – we were best friends."

"Maddie," she introduced herself. "Did Joan have any enemies, or problems with anyone?"

"No." The woman looked at her with wide eyes. "Not that I know of. Why do you ask?"

"I was just wondering if that might have something to do with her murder," Maddie said, her voice low.

"I never thought of that." Linda clapped a hand to her mouth and closed her eyes in apparent thought. "No, I can't think of anything troubling her. She had mentioned her husband was thinking of retiring soon, but that was a few weeks ago."

"How did she feel about that?" Maddie probed.

"Well, let's see …" The woman shook her head. "We were close, but sometimes I don't think she told me everything, just like I don't – didn't – tell her everything. You know, little things that are just between a husband and wife. That sort of thing. So when she told me her husband was talking about early retirement, she didn't sound upset about it, really."

"Did she sound happy about it?"

Linda pursed her lips. "She didn't sound ecstatic about it. But she'd just mentioned it in passing. I didn't think afterward, *Joan doesn't sound thrilled about that.*"

Maddie nodded. "Does – did Joan work?"

"Oh, no. She said they were quite comfortably off with her husband Brian's job. I know their house is paid for, so they don't have to worry about making rent or mortgage payments."

"I see." Maddie paused, not sure what to ask next.

"Why do you want to know all this?" Linda asked. "The detective said they're going to do their best to find out who did it."

"That's good," Maddie replied. "Joan was one of my regulars, and I saw her yesterday morning. I just can't believe this happened." And she couldn't. If only she'd warned Joan in a much more specific way, instead of just telling her to be "careful".

"I know." Linda shook her head in sorrow. "If only I hadn't cancelled our jog this morning."

***

On her walk back to the coffee truck, there was one recurring thought in Maddie's mind – Linda hadn't looked sick at all, apart from her tear-blotched face. Yet she'd used that excuse to cancel her morning jog with Joan.

Was Maddie imagining things, or was there a reason to suspect Linda?

"Where did you go?" Suzanne asked as Maddie climbed back into the truck, banging the door behind her.

"To ask Linda some questions." At Suzanne's blank look, she elaborated, "Joan's neighbor and best friend who ordered that black coffee."

"Oh." Suzanne nodded. "So, what did she say?"

"Not much." Maddie frowned. "Only that she cancelled going jogging with Joan this morning because she wasn't feeling well."

Suzanne wrinkled up her nose. "I can't say I blame her. I'd hate to go running at the crack of dawn."

Maddie tapped her lip. "How long have we been here, on the town square?"

"Six months. Why?"

"Yet I can't remember ever seeing Joan or her neighbor Linda out jogging in the morning."

"You're right." Suzanne snapped her fingers.

"So did they really go jogging together – apart from this morning? Or is the word *jogging* a cover for something else they did together?"

"Like what?" Suzanne's eyes widened. "Sneaking out of the house to do something that their husbands don't know about? Yoga with a hot male instructor? Bootcamp with a hot male instructor? I know! They both had hot male lovers and this was the only time they could meet them!"

Maddie made a face. "At seven a.m.?"

"Think about it," Suzanne urged. "Jogging would be a great cover for meeting your boyfriend on the side."

"But both women look like they're in their fifties," Maddie pointed out.

"So? Just because you're older doesn't mean you're dead inside."

"Says the twenty-seven-year-old woman," Maddie teased, "who seems to have hot males on the brain."

"What can I say?" Suzanne sighed. "It's been a while. And maybe there should be some yoga classes around here with a hunky guy showing you the poses. I would definitely go." She nudged Maddie. "And I bet you would, too."

"Probably," Maddie conceded. Just like Suzanne had said, it had been a while for her, too. But right now she was busy with her burgeoning coffee truck business, and trying to discover if there was more than one spell she could do. But, if casting spells meant she could foresee someone's death, she didn't want to do that anymore.

So why even bother trying to see if she could cast different spells from the old witchcraft book now that she had turned twenty-seven?

"What are you going to do now?" Suzanne asked.

"Speak to Joan's husband, I guess."

"Are you sure you want to do this?" Suzanne asked.

"I'm sure." Maddie nodded. But she wasn't certain at all. Only the guilt she felt at seeing the vision in the coffee cup compelled her to continue with her investigation.

"Then I suppose you should visit Joan's husband," Suzanne said.

"Yes." Maddie took out her phone, pressed a button, and showed the screen to Suzanne. "But first, look what Trixie is up to."

"Ohhh." Suzanne smiled as she watched the white Persian sit on the sofa next to the ancient book on witchcraft in Maddie's living room.

Maddie had installed a camera connected to her Wi-Fi connection and her phone a few months ago. On the days when Trixie didn't accompany her to work, Maddie liked knowing what the feline got up to when she wasn't around.

"Wouldn't it be cool if she could open the book and flip through the pages?" Suzanne giggled.

"Something tells me she might have done that already." Maddie smiled, the sight of the cat lifting her mood.

"Really?" Suzanne raised her eyebrows.

"Uh-huh." Maddie nodded. "One day I came home and I could have sworn the book was shut when I left that morning. But it was wide open, and Trixie was staring at the page, as if she was actually reading it."

"You're definitely a witch." Suzanne nodded. "Your powers just aren't at their fullest yet, that's all."

"Maybe I don't want them to be," Maddie said somberly. "Look what happened yesterday – and this morning. If I hadn't done that spell with Joan's coffee—"

"But something made you do it, right?" Suzanne asked. "You told me a while ago that you get a feeling for when to do it for other people."

"Yes," Maddie said reluctantly.

"What if you were supposed to do it yesterday? So you could see Joan's murder? What if you're supposed to solve it?"

"Do you think so?" Maddie asked after a pause.

"Yeah." Suzanne said. "It makes sense to me. I know you feel horrible right now about it all, but what if someone out there—" she waved a hand in the air to indicate the air, the universe, or heaven – or maybe all three "—has decided you could use your power for good?"

"It's not as if I'm using it for evil," Maddie said wryly.

"But doing something with it that's bigger than you or me," Suzanne said impatiently. "Helping to balance the random cosmicness of everything."

Maddie knitted her brow. "Since when did you become all woo-woo?"

Suzanne flushed. "I've been reading some books from the library. Think about it, Maddie. What if for some reason the sheriff's department can't solve the murder, but you can? But if you hadn't cast the spell on Joan's coffee, you mightn't have felt the urge to investigate."

Or, on the other hand, Maddie thought, I might have felt guilty that I hadn't done the spell to sneak a peek at Joan's future and I would have still felt compelled to investigate. But she decided to keep that thought to herself. Suzanne was on a roll.

"Let's go and see Joan's husband. The library should be open by now," Suzanne said.

CHAPTER 5

"Do you really think Joan's husband will be at the library today?" Maddie asked as they walked across the town square to the nutmeg brown brick building.

They'd locked up the coffee truck and had posted a note on the serving window saying they would be back in thirty minutes.

This was the first time they'd left the truck unattended. Maddie hoped it would be the last. Although business was good at the moment, if they kept leaving the coffee truck to go sleuthing, there wouldn't be a business left!

"I don't know," Suzanne replied. "But if he isn't here, he's sure to be at home."

They entered through the automatic sliding glass doors, walls and walls of books greeting them. At the desk, a tall, slim woman in her early thirties, wearing a pair of silver wire-rimmed glasses, her mousy brown hair in a slightly untidy up do, checked in library books. She held a scanner over each barcode, a low *beep* emitting after each book passed through her hands.

"Can I help you?" She looked up at Maddie and Suzanne.

"Is Mr. Hodgeton here?" Maddie asked.

"No." The woman shook her head. "He's taking some personal time."

"We heard what happened this morning," Suzanne said, her voice low, matching the librarian's. "We're very sorry."

"Thank you." The librarian nodded. "I'm not sure when Bri – Mr. Hodgeton will be back."

"Are you in charge while he's not here?" Maddie asked. "I knew his wife—" she hoped she wasn't flushing at the lie – although she had known Joan, it wasn't very well – "—and I was told he was the head librarian here."

"He is." The woman nodded. "And yes, as the library assistant, I'll be in charge in his absence. As you can see—" she nodded at the large room "—this is only a relatively small library."

Maddie spied her white name badge, hidden amongst the white and pale pink floral pattern of her blouse – *Phoebe Halpern.*

"Are there any other staff besides you and Mr. Hodgeton?" Maddie asked.

"A volunteer comes in two days per week," Phoebe replied, "but this isn't one of her days."

Suzanne peered at the library assistant's neckline. "That's a pretty locket."

"This?" The library assistant flushed, fingering the small gold necklace dangling down, lying against the fabric of her blouse. "It's just a little something I treated myself to."

"It's very nice," Suzanne said.

"Thank you."

They both watched as Phoebe tucked the locket inside her neckline.

"More professional." She smiled at them, but was there a hint of strain in the smile? Or was Maddie imagining things?

"We wanted to pay our respects to Mr. Hodgeton," Maddie said. "Do you think he'll be at home?"

"Probably." The library assistant nodded. "The sheriff's office was questioning him this morning."

"They were?" Suzanne asked.

"Yes." Phoebe shook her head. "As if Brian would do such a thing! They should looking for the real killer, not hounding librarians." Her bosom heaved, and a flush of indignation spread over her face.

"I hope they do catch the person responsible," Maddie said sincerely.

Maddie and Suzanne departed the library. Once they were outside, Suzanne turned to Maddie.

"Did you see the initials on her locket?" she asked in a whisper, although there was nobody near them on the street.

"Not really. You were closer to it than me. I noticed you peering at it," Maddie replied.

"The initials on the locket are the same as Brian's – Joan's husband! BH." Excitement flickered across Suzanne's face.

"Are you sure?" Maddie demanded.

"Yes. That's why I had such a good look at it," Suzanne replied. "Do you know what this means? Phoebe, the library assistant, is in love with Joan's husband!"

"It could mean that," Maddie agreed slowly. "Or it could mean that she has a

47

boyfriend with the same initials, or it might even be her mother's or another family member's initials and she's wearing it as a keepsake."

Suzanne looked at her skeptically. "She works with him and calls him by his first name. You heard how it slipped out. And look how passionate she got about him being innocent at the end."

"Yeah." Maddie nodded. "I did think her reaction was a little over the top, but …"

"I'm sure she's in love with him," Suzanne insisted as they walked back to the coffee truck.

"He must be older than her," Maddie pointed out. "If he's around the same age as Joan, and talking about retiring early, he must be at least fifteen years her senior."

"So? Maybe she likes older men."

"And he's married."

"Not anymore."

"Yeah." Maddie's voice held a note of sadness. "Not anymore."

They reached the truck. There were no customers waiting for them to open.

"Come on," Suzanne urged. "Let's go and talk to Brian."

Maddie raised an eyebrow. "We don't want to miss the lunch hour rush."

"I know it's one of our busiest times, but after seeing the library assistant wig out like that, I really think we should talk to Brian ASAP."

"Are you sure you don't want to take over the whole investigation?" Maddie asked wryly. "You seem keener than I am to solve Joan's murder."

"Sorry." Suzanne looked apologetic. "It's just that it was interesting talking to Phoebe, the library assistant, and I think it's right that we're – you're – investigating Joan's death."

"*We* are," Maddie confirmed. "Okay," she blew out a breath, "let's go and talk to Joan's husband. And then we're coming back here and serving the customers we have left."

"Deal." Suzanne smiled. "Let's go."

CHAPTER 6

Maddie rang the brass doorbell.

Ding dong.

The street was quiet. Nobody ran or walked past. The other houses were similar to this one – well-kept brick houses with neat green lawns. In fact, you couldn't even tell that there had been a murder committed here this morning.

An icy shiver ran down her spine at the thought.

"Do you think he's home?" Suzanne whispered.

"If he doesn't answer in a few minutes, we'd better go back to the truck," Maddie replied, checking the time on her watch. If they didn't leave soon, they'd miss the whole of the lunch hour, and their customers.

In the next second, the door creaked open. A middle-aged man with bloodshot eyes and a strained face greeted them.

"This isn't a good time," he said shortly.

"I'm sorry, Mr. Hodgeton," Maddie said. "We heard about your wife and just wanted to pay our respects."

The expression on Mr. Hodgeton's face softened.

"Come in. I can offer you coffee or tea. Or juice," he added over his shoulder as he led the way into the living room.

"How did you know Joan?" he asked once they'd all taken a seat. Two tan sofas faced each other, forming a conversation nook in the cream and gray accented room.

"We run the coffee truck on the town square," Maddie said, wondering if he would throw them out the minute he heard they weren't close friends of his wife's.

"In fact, she ordered a coffee yesterday," Suzanne jumped in. "Her usual spiced latte. She always told Maddie how great her coffee was."

"You're the coffee girl." Mr. Hodgeton pointed his finger at Maddie. "Yes, Joanie mentioned your coffee to me, said I had to try it one day." He looked toward the kitchen. "Would you girls like something to drink?"

"No, thank you, Mr. Hodgeton," Maddie said. "We don't want to keep you. I imagine you must be busy with … everything." She didn't know what else to say. What does one say to a man whose wife has just been murdered?

"Call me Brian. Yeah." He smiled without humor. "A detective questioned me this morning. What was I doing home? Why had my wife cancelled her morning jog?" He drummed his fingers on his knee. "They should be looking for the real killer, instead of asking me ridiculous questions."

"We met Joan's friend this morning," Maddie said. "Linda?"

"She lives next door. With her husband," he said. "They were – are – good friends. She even has a key to our house, for emergencies, and we – I – have a key for theirs. She and Joan used to go jogging regularly, but Linda called this morning and cancelled. Said she wasn't feeling well."

Why hadn't Linda told them she had a key to Joan's house? Maddie furrowed her brow.

"That's what Linda told us," Suzanne said.

"If she hadn't cancelled ..." he let the thought trail off, then shrugged wearily. "But who knows? The maniac might have killed Joan while she was out jogging, and maybe Linda, too."

"We get a lot of joggers buying water from us in the morning," Maddie said. "But I can't remember seeing Joan and Linda jogging around the town square."

"No. They just jogged around the block here a few times," Brian informed them. "Joan said once she didn't want everyone to see her looking hot and sweaty."

"Does the detective think there's a motive behind it?" Maddie asked delicately.

Brian snorted. "If he does, he hasn't shared his thoughts with me. Instead, they treat me like a criminal, just because I forgot to get the meat out for dinner."

"Oh?" Maddie hoped her tone sounded encouraging.

"Yes. It was my turn to cook dinner tonight, so I'd decided to fix beef bourgignon. But before I left the house, I'd forgotten to get the meat out. So before

53

I could start work at the library, I had to come home and pull the beef out of the freezer, so it could defrost in time for tonight. And that's when I saw—" he ran a hand over his face. "There was water and roses everywhere, as well as glass. Poor Joan."

"You went somewhere on the way to the library?" Maddie probed.

"I met with my library assistant before work." He waved it off as if it were no big deal. "I had an idea for this big charity project that would help the library, as well as kids who can't read, and I wanted to talk to her about it, see if she would support me, before I ran it past the board of directors. Sometimes it's so busy at the library, there's not much time to talk about stuff like that. So I met her before work this morning."

"Where did you meet?" Suzanne asked curiously.

"At her apartment." He leaned back in his armchair. "In case you're wondering, Joan knew about it and was fine about the whole thing. She's met my library assistant and thinks – thought—" his voice faltered "—that Phoebe is a great girl. Very dedicated to her job."

"Do you think the charity project will go ahead?" Maddie asked.

"I hope so." He sounded sincere. "There are too many kids who don't know how to read. I thought I could get this project going before I retired."

"Linda said you were thinking of retiring soon," Suzanne commented.

"Yes." He sighed. "But I don't know what's going to happen now. There's the funeral to plan—" his voice cracked "—and then I'm expected to go back to work as if nothing happened." He shook his head. "I just don't know what I'm going to do."

Maddie couldn't think of any more questions to ask him, and apparently neither could Suzanne, as she remained silent. They thanked Brian, and left the house.

"Poor guy," Suzanne said as they walked down the street. "He does seem broken up."

"Mmm," Maddie agreed. "Did you hear him say that Linda has a key to the house? She didn't tell us that earlier."

"You're right." Suzanne stopped and turned to face Maddie. "She didn't."

"*And* she cancelled their regular jogging session," Maddie continued.

Just then, a sheriff's vehicle pulled up at the curb. A portly man in his sixties clambered out of the car and walked over to them.

"Excuse me," he said politely, standing right in front of them. His gray hair was more salt than pepper, and his brown gaze fixed on them intently. He was dressed in plain clothes – a worn brown suit with a white shirt and navy tie slightly askew at the neck.

"Don't you run the coffee truck in the town square?" he asked Maddie.

"Yes sir," she replied.

"Detective Edgewater. Don't go too far. I'll want to talk to you later." He pulled out his wallet and flashed a badge at them. "Apparently, you served Joan Hodgeton coffee yesterday morning."

"That's right," Maddie replied, wondering why he wanted to talk to them.

"How do you know that?" Suzanne blurted out.

"People talk." He tapped his old-fashioned notebook peeking out of his top pocket of his suit jacket. "What are you two doing here instead of working out of your truck?"

"Paying our condolences," Maddie replied.

"As long as that's all it is," the detective said sternly. "I don't want any amateurs poking their nose into this business. I know what people get up to, reading the latest mystery on the bestseller list and thinking they can do a better job than law enforcement. You leave this to the professionals."

"Yes, sir." Maddie nodded. What else could she say?

"I'll see you girls later." The man passed them and walked up to the Hodgeton's house.

"Wow," Suzanne whispered once they were out of earshot. "What got up his butt?"

"Suze!" Maddie kept her voice low, stifling a giggle. "Don't let him hear you say that."

"I won't." Suzanne cast a glance over her shoulder, as if she suddenly thought the detective had heard her after all, but the house was now in the distance.

"Do you think he's right?" Maddie asked soberly as they turned into the town square. "Should we keep investigating?"

"Of course we should!" Suzanne said confidently. "Don't let him scare you off, Mads."

"You're right," Maddie replied, giving herself a mental shake. She'd been determined earlier today to investigate Joan's death, and she wasn't going to let anything stop her – not her own doubts as to her sleuthing ability, or warnings from law enforcement. What harm could happen from asking people a few questions?

They unlocked the truck and opened for business. People were already sitting on benches in the park, enjoying their lunch from home, or what they had bought from the sandwich shop nearby, or the burger place.

After a few minutes, their first lunchtime customer stepped up to the window, and soon Maddie and Suzanne were busy serving coffee.

Finally, people returned to work, and Maddie and Suzanne flopped down on their stools in the truck.

"Phew!" Suzanne dramatically mopped her brow. "That was intense."

"Precisely why I don't want us to close the truck for too long while we're asking questions," Maddie replied. "Otherwise we'll lose too much business."

"I know, Mads." Suzanne nodded in agreement. "We don't want any of our customers needing caffeine so badly they go to the *coffee shop*."

Maddie made a face. "I seriously don't know how Claudine is still operating. That coffee is truly awful."

"And so are her pastries," Suzanne said. "That's why I thought making our own cookies would be a good idea, but now I think making health balls will be even better. Less work and more profit. And it's something that Claudine at the coffee shop doesn't sell – at least not the last time I was in there."

"And when was that?" Maddie raised an eyebrow in jest. "I hope you're not thinking of defecting to the competition."

59

"Just checking her out. I popped in last week during our lunch break. I was going to tell you, but then we got slammed in the afternoon and I completely forgot. You should have seen the expressions on some of her customer's faces as they left. They obviously *did not* have a good experience."

"I can't believe I lasted so long there once Claudine took over," Maddie said.

"I'm glad you quit," Suzanne said. "This is so much better than working there, isn't it?"

"You bet." Maddie grinned at her best friend.

"No customers?" A whining, nasal voice assaulted their ears. A stout forty-something woman with jet black hair cropped short stepped up to the counter and peered over it, as if cataloging everything she could see in the truck.

Maddie and Suzanne sprang to their feet.

"Can I help you with something, Claudine?" Maddie asked politely, hoping her former boss hadn't overheard her conversation with Suzanne.

"Just seeing how business is, girls."
Claudine smirked. "I got some new
customers today. Imagine my surprise
when they said the coffee truck was
closed. Thought I'd come and check up on
you two."

"Thanks for your concern," Suzanne
said coolly. "But as you can see—" she
waved a hand around the truck, "—we're
fine."

"Uh-huh." Maddie's former boss did
not sound convinced. "Well, once my new
customers have experienced *my* coffee,
they'll definitely be coming back for
more." She tsked. "I didn't think your
coffee van idea would work at all, Maddie,
but now more people have tasted *my*
superior coffee, I doubt they'll be visiting
you again."

Claudine peered at the counter.

"What, no cookies or pastries?"

"When coffee is as good as Maddie's,
you don't need gimmicks like that."
Suzanne's eyes flashed at the older
woman.

"Ha! You'll find out," Claudine
warned, wagging a finger at them.

"Find out what?" Maddie asked politely, inwardly seething.

"That you'll need to sell more than coffee to make a living," Claudine spelled out, as if Maddie were a five-year-old. "Plus, you'll need the proper permits to make anything extra apart from coffee drinks," she added. "Do you have such a permit?"

"That's our business," Maddie said, standing her ground.

Suzanne nodded, looking like she was trying to stop herself from blurting out something rude.

"I've got my eye on you girls," Claudine said, taking one step back.

Suddenly, Claudine didn't look or sound as confident as she had a second ago. Maddie didn't know if it was because of the combined glare she and Suzanne were giving her former boss, or if perhaps a little of her coffee witch power had kicked in without her realizing it. Whatever it was, Claudine was now backing off.

"I've got customers to attend to!" The important announcement sounded wavery.

Claudine turned on her heel and trotted back toward her coffee shop.

Suzanne blew out a deep breath. "What was that all about?"

"I have no idea." Maddie shrugged.

"How can she think any new customers will come back for more of her awful coffee? And I'm sorry some of ours went to her shop today, but there's no comparison between your coffee and hers."

"Thanks." Maddie smiled at Suzanne. "But do you think she's right about needing a permit to sell cookies or even the health balls you were talking about?"

"No." Suzanne shook her head. "I looked into it. We should be perfectly fine making the health balls with the permit we have now. We can go to the supermarket after work and buy the ingredients to make them, and tomorrow we can wow our customers with them."

"Sounds like a plan." They high-fived each other.

Before they could make themselves an afternoon latte, the same detective lumbered up to the truck.

"Detective." Maddie nodded at him. "How can I help you?" It never hurt to be polite, especially to law enforcement.

"I've been told that Joan Hodgeton ordered a coffee here yesterday." He took out his notebook and pencil.

"Yes, that's right," Maddie replied.

After Maddie and Suzanne gave him their names and addresses, he continued: "What did you give her?"

"Her usual spiced latte."

"What was in it?"

"Coffee, milk, cinnamon, and nutmeg," Maddie answered.

"Did you serve her anything else?"

"We don't sell anything besides coffee, tea, or bottled water," Suzanne said.

"I see." He eyed what he could see of the interior of the food truck. "No pastries?"

"No," Maddie replied.

"Huh." He looked perplexed for a minute. "And you make a living doing that?"

"Yes," Maddie replied. In fact, she made more with her truck, splitting everything fifty-fifty with Suzanne after expenses, than she had at the coffee shop, before and after Claudine took over.

"We're planning on trying a new line of health balls tomorrow, detective," Suzanne offered. "Full of goodness. Coconut, dates, cacao, that kind of thing."

"Huh." The man looked more perplexed than ever, then dropped his gaze to his notebook. "Now, let's see. Did Joan Hodgeton seem troubled at all? Did she say anything to you?"

"No, she didn't say anything to me," Maddie said slowly, not wanting to lie. "Apart from placing her order." How could she tell this detective about the vision she'd seen in the coffee cup? He'd probably either laugh at her, or try to have her locked up for wasting his time, or worse.

"What was her mood like?" he persisted.

"The same as usual, really," Maddie replied. "Maybe a little down."

"Hmm." He wrote something in his notebook. "And did she stay here long?"

"No," Maddie said. "She took her coffee and left."

"You didn't see her talk to anyone when she left the truck?"

"No." Maddie shook her head.

"No," Suzanne said.

"Thanks." He sighed heavily. "That's all for now. But in case I need to talk to you again, do you always park here?"

"Yes," Maddie replied. "This is our usual spot."

"Would you like to try our coffee, sir?" Suzanne asked. "It's the best in town."

"You wouldn't be trying to bribe me, would you?" he frowned.

"No, detective. You'd have to pay full price just like everyone else," Suzanne replied seriously.

He barked with laughter. "Okay, show me what you've got." He pulled out his wallet. "How much for a black coffee?"

"You don't want a cappuccino or a latte, or a mocha?" Maddie asked, disappointed with his no frills order. She loved trying to convert sceptics into satisfied customers with her specialties.

"I'm not a fancy kind of guy." He indicated his worn suit. "In case you haven't noticed, I still use a notebook and pencil, not a tablet connected to Wi-Fi, to write down my notes."

"We did notice that," Suzanne said politely.

"Okay." He paused. "Give me a fancy cappuccino." He pulled some bills from his wallet. "That will probably cost double what a black coffee would, right?"

"Almost," Maddie replied. She indicated the bottles of flavored syrups near the machine. "Which flavor would you like? Caramel, hazelnut—"

"Surprise me."

"Okay." Maddie set to work, determined to make the detective the best cappuccino she could. Surveying the syrup bottles, she decided on vanilla. Detective Edgewater appeared to be a no-nonsense guy, and would probably deem vanilla as an acceptable flavor.

Grinding and hissing ensued, before Maddie finished off his drink with her signature art – an image of Trixie. "Here you go. That's $4.40 please."

A look of surprise crossed his face. "No wonder you girls are making a living at this." He pushed the cash across the counter.

Maddie handed him his change.

"Well?" Suzanne looked at him expectantly. "Aren't you going to try it?"

"Give me a minute." He looked down at his drink. "That's clever how you've made a pattern of a cat with the foam on top."

"We think so." Suzanne smiled at him.

"Would you like me to put a lid on it?" Maddie asked.

"No, no, this is fine." He raised the cup to his lips and took a tentative sip. His expression turned into one of pleasure. "Not bad. Not bad at all."

"It's better than not bad," Suzanne muttered under her breath.

"I'm glad you like it," Maddie said, wondering if he would now become one of their regulars. "I added a vanilla syrup to the coffee base."

"Vanilla," he repeated, taking another sip. "Yeah, I can taste that." He nodded.

After he drank a little more, he cleared his throat.

"Remember what I said to you two before, back at Mr. Hodgeton's house. I don't want any members of the public interfering in the case. You let the professionals handle this. Are we clear?"

"Yes," Maddie said slowly. What else could she say?

When Suzanne remained silent, they both looked at her.

"But what if you can't solve it?" she burst out.

"We will," the detective said, taking another sip of his cappuccino. "From what I've gathered, Joan was one of your customers, but you didn't have a close, personal friendship with her, did you?" He eyed both of them in turn, as if daring them to lie to him.

"No, sir," Maddie replied. "She was a regular customer, and I liked her, but I didn't see her outside the truck." She waved her hand as if to indicated that "outside" meant outside the confines of the town square and serving coffee.

"No-o-o," Suzanne finally answered.

"Okay, now." He took another swallow of coffee. "You girls keep making good coffee like this, and stay out of trouble. And maybe I'll come back tomorrow and try one of these health balls you told me about. Full price, of course," he added.

"Yes, sir." Suzanne saluted him.

He shook his head in mock disbelief and walked back to his vehicle.

CHAPTER 7

"I can't believe he called us "girls"",
Suzanne murmured once he appeared out
of earshot.

"I know," Maddie agreed. "But it's not
as if we're middle-aged. Maybe we're too
young for ma'am, and miss would sound
weird, right?"

"Yeah," Suzanne said with feeling.
"But we don't look like teenagers, do
we?"

"I hope not." Maddie grabbed a bottle
of water and unscrewed the cap. "But we
don't look old for twenty-seven, do we?"

"No way!"

They flopped onto their stools. Maddie
checked her phone, looking at Trixie the
cat on the screen.

"What's Trixie doing now?" Suzanne
inquired, peering over Maddie's shoulder.

"Still sitting next to the spell book."
Maddie furrowed her brow. "I wonder if
she's been there since earlier this
morning."

"Maybe she's waiting for you to come home so you can try casting a new spell," Suzanne suggested.

Maddie yawned. "When I get home, all I'll feel like doing is relaxing on the couch and watching TV."

Suzanne looked at her watch. "It's 3.30. If we close up early, we could buy the ingredients for the health balls and start earlier tomorrow, so the balls will be ready by the time our first customer arrives."

Maddie looked out across the square. Only a couple of people sat on the park benches, either reading a newspaper or looking at their phone.

"I guess. We don't get many people between now and four, anyway."

"I've already made a list of the ingredients we need." Suzanne jumped up from her stool.

After they closed up the truck and deposited the day's takings in the bank across the square, it was almost four.

"We can keep the ingredients in the truck," Suzanne said, as they walked to the small supermarket just off the square.

"And when I get home, I'll put my food processor into the truck, ready for tomorrow."

"Our goodies are going to blow Claudine's paltry offerings out of the water," Suzanne declared.

Maddie had seen the type of health balls Suzanne was enthusiastic about in health food stores, but to her knowledge, no shops near the town square sold them. She hadn't tried one, either.

"These balls are going to taste good, aren't they?" she asked as they entered the grocery store.

"Everyone raves about them online," Suzanne assured her, grabbing a cart and digging out her list.

"Have you tried them?" Maddie asked.

"Well, not exactly," Suzanne murmured.

"Suze!"

"I was going to make a small batch for us, so we could snack on them during the day, but then I thought we might as well make a large batch and sell them to customers so we can recoup our costs right from the start."

"What if they don't work out? Or don't taste very nice?" Maddie asked.

"They will, Mads." Suzanne touched her arm. "You've got to have faith."

Maddie absorbed her friend's words as they collected the ingredients they needed. Suzanne was right – sometimes Maddie doubted herself. Not in her ability to make coffee – she was confident she had the right skillset there – but in other areas of her life, such as her supposed witchy powers and non-existent love life.

They paid for the healthy ingredients at the check-out: coconut, cacao, fresh dates, and almond meal.

Maddie raised her eyebrows at the total – healthy food was expensive – but pulled out her wallet without a murmur.

Suzanne had supported her idea of running a coffee truck; the least she could do was support her friend's idea of adding a profitable sideline to their business.

"The balls will take an hour to set," Suzanne informed her as they walked back to the truck. "So if we park in the square an hour earlier than normal, they should be almost ready by 7.30, when the first lot of regulars arrive."

Maddie stopped in her tracks and stared at her friend.

"Are you crazy? It's difficult for me to get up at 6.30 as it is – you want me to get up one hour earlier?"

"Yeah, I didn't know if you'd be happy about that." Suzanne blew out a breath. "But I'm really excited about this idea. And I thought if our first batch was a hit, we could make a second batch for the lunch hour rush."

Maddie frowned. "How many balls will we make from one batch? And what is our profit going to be on each ball?"

"We can make a large batch of forty, and we should make at least one dollar profit on each ball. So if we sell forty per day—"

"That's two-hundred dollars extra per week, plus however many we sell Saturday morning."

Maddie and Suzanne parked the coffee truck at the town square on Saturday mornings as well, closing at lunchtime. That gave them one and a half days to relax and have fun, before starting work again on Monday mornings.

"Okay." Maddie sighed. "Six-thirty tomorrow. But," she warned, "there's no way I'll be getting up one hour earlier every day."

"I know." Suzanne nodded. "Once I get a system sorted out, I can probably make them during our slow times, and you won't have to get out of bed any earlier."

"Deal." They smiled at each other, then stored the ingredients in the truck.

Maddie dropped off Suzanne at her house nearby, then headed home.

It had been a long day. First, the news about Joan, then her investigating Joan's death. *And* being warned off by law enforcement.

She parked the truck and unlocked her front door, her thoughts busy with everything they had learned that day.

"Trixie!" She pushed open the wooden door, a creak sounding in the air. No matter how many times she applied olive oil to the hinges, the door still creaked when she arrived home every day.

Her fluffy Persian trotted down the hall to greet her.

"Mrrow."

"What have you been up to today?" Maddie bent to stroke the feline.

"Mrrow. Mrrow." Trixie looked up at her expectantly.

"I saw you sitting next to the spell book," Maddie told her, wondering if her cat minded being filmed when she was alone in the house.

"Mrrow." The Persian rubbed her face against Maddie's leg.

"All right." Maddie put her purse down on the side table in the hall and followed Trixie into the living room. "Do you want to show me something?"

Trixie hopped up on the sofa right next to the spell book, looking at Maddie.

"Okay." Maddie sat on the other side of the open book and studied the two pages.

"How to discover if someone is telling the truth," she read out slowly.

"Mrrow!"

"You want me to try this spell?"

"Mrrow!" Trixie nudged her arm from across the book.

"Well, okay," Maddie said. She read the spell thoroughly. If she could master it, it would help with her investigation into Joan's death.

"It says I need to cast it when I'm talking to someone and I want to know if they're lying to me or not," she told the feline. "So I'm going to have to memorize the words – I can't exactly carrying this big heavy book around with me."

Trixie made a raspy noise that sounded like "No."

Maddie nodded, wondering not for the first time if she was crazy for talking to her cat as if Trixie could understand every word Maddie said.

But why couldn't Trixie do that? Her unusual turquoise eyes gleamed with intelligence, and her silver spine and tail made her stand out from a regular cat.

If Maddie was truly a witch, then why couldn't Trixie be her familiar, and have the ability to understand human speech?

And besides, she enjoyed talking to Trixie as if the Persian could understand her.

"Maybe I should write this down, Trix." Maddie jumped up and grabbed a pen and note pad from the kitchen, and returned.

After writing down the spell, she read it silently again, then nodded.

"I'll give this a try tomorrow, if I ask more questions about Joan," she told Trixie, folding up the piece of paper and tucking it into her purse in the hall.

"Mrrow," the cat said approvingly.

"We're going to have to get up early tomorrow," she told the cat. "Suzanne wants to make health balls before our first customers arrive."

"Broomf!" Trixie's face scrunched up in disapproval.

"You don't have to get up with me," she reassured her. "You can stay home again tomorrow if you want."

Trixie closed her eyes, as if thinking about it. Finally, she let out a grudging, "Mrrow."

It seemed Trixie would be joining them tomorrow.

CHAPTER 8

"The health balls will be ready in thirty minutes!" Suzanne called out.

Maddie grunted in reply, struggling to open her eyes. As soon as she'd parked the truck in the square that morning, she'd made herself a super strong espresso, but even that hadn't been enough to stop her eyelids from closing. She had dozed on her stool in the truck, half listening to the whizzing and whirring as her partner made the health balls in the food processor.

Trixie had insisted on coming this morning, although she seemed a little grumpy, too, at the early hour.

"Sorry." Maddie opened her eyes and looked at Suzanne. "I haven't been much help this morning."

"No worries." Suzanne smiled at her, looking positively cheery. "Once you taste them, you'll know they're going to be a best seller. And," she continued, looking excited, "you can try the first one!"

"You should," Maddie replied. "They're your idea."

"But I want you to," Suzanne said. "They're full of healthy ingredients and might give you some extra energy."

"As long as you take the second bite," Maddie insisted.

"Mrrow." Trixie sounded as if she agreed with Maddie.

"Okay, Trixie." Suzanne giggled.

A knock sounded on the glass window. They hadn't opened up the counter for business yet, since they were at their spot earlier than usual and hadn't expected any premature customers.

Maddie and Suzanne exchanged a glance, then Maddie hopped up and unlocked the window.

"Are you open yet?" A senior citizen whose bobbed gray hair was tinged with a pink rinse, peered up at her. She wore a pink blouse and skirt and carried a black handbag.

Maddie recognized her as one of their semi-regulars, but she usually arrived mid-morning.

"What would you like?" Maddie smiled.

"One of your wonderful cappuccinos, please," the elderly woman said, rummaging in her capacious purse for her wallet. "Thank goodness you're here already! I had a terrible coffee yesterday when you'd closed the truck—" she peered at them curiously "—from that coffee shop over there." She pointed a finger at Claudine's café on the far side of the square. She shuddered. "Never again."

"I'll get it started for you." Maddie poured some beans into the machine, the sound of grinding filling the air.

Suzanne took the customer's money and gave her change.

"You girls aren't usually here this early, are you?" the senior continued.

"No, ma'am." Suzanne's tone was upbeat. "But we're introducing a new sideline – health balls. They'll be ready soon if you'd like to come back and try one."

"What's that?" The woman's nose wrinkled.

"They're full of goodness," Suzanne said enthusiastically. "They've got coconut, dates, almond meal, and cacao in them."

"I don't know …" the senior said hesitantly. "I don't know if I'd like it. On the other hand, they can't be worse than that horrible cookie I had at the coffee shop yesterday." She shuddered and lowered her voice. "I think it was stale!"

"Our goodies are made today," Suzanne said. "And the dates are fresh, not dried."

"Maybe I'll come back, then," the senior said, as Maddie handed her the paper cup. "Thank you, dear." She took the cappuccino, sipping it briefly. "Delicious as always."

"Thanks." Maddie smiled at the elderly customer.

"Where were you girls yesterday? I was disappointed that you were closed."

Maddie hesitated. What should she say? That they'd been investigating the death of one of their regular customers?

But before she could answer, the old lady continued, "It was terrible news about Joan's death, wasn't it?"

"Did you know her?" Maddie asked.

"Mm-hm." The senior nodded. "We did some fund-raising a while ago for starving children in Africa. She seemed a very nice woman."

"I thought so, too," Maddie replied. "She was one of our regulars."

"It doesn't surprise me, dear. Your coffee is wonderful."

"Thank you," Maddie said again.

The old lady shook her head. "I don't know what her husband is going to do without her. And her neighbor! They were very close, I believe."

"Do you mean Linda?" Suzanne asked.

"Yes, Linda." The woman leaned forward, although there was no one else around, and lowered her voice. "I saw her going into that massage parlor yesterday, the day Joan died! I don't know what her husband would say if he found out."

"Massage parlor?" Maddie and Suzanne said at the same time.

The elderly woman nodded. "I saw him once standing in the doorway. Very handsome in a European way, if you know what I mean. And I'm sure he's younger than Linda. Why, she must be fifty-five if she's a day. So what was she doing going in there, that's what I'd like to know."

"Um, getting a legit massage?" Suzanne offered. "That's the tiny store squeezed into the corner of the square, isn't it?"

"That's right, dear." The senior took another sip of her cappuccino. "You have to go *upstairs.*" The last word was spoken in a hushed whisper.

"What time yesterday morning?" Maddie knitted her brow. Hadn't Linda told them she'd been unwell and had cancelled her jog with Joan?

"It was quite early." The elderly woman shook her head. "Too early for hanky-panky, if you ask me. Even if he is devilishly good looking."

Before they could ask the senior any more questions, a sudden influx of people crowded around the truck.

"Don't let me keep you, girls." The old lady toddled off toward the other side of the square.

Maddie and Suzanne were so busy keeping up with orders, Trixie "helping" by dozing on one of the stools, that it was almost an hour before they caught their breath.

"Drat!" Suzanne made a sound of exasperation. "We were so busy I forgot all about the balls!"

"Let's try them now," Maddie replied, feeling brave.

Suzanne took them out of the small refrigerator. Forty balls coated with shredded coconut covered the tray.

Suzanne checked her watch. "They should be more than ready now."

She offered the tray to Maddie before taking one herself.

"Don't forget, you get the first bite."

Maddie nodded, then bit into it tentatively. An explosion of texture and taste tingled her taste buds. Dates, chocolate, coconut. To her surprise, she took another small bite, and another, until the morsel disappeared.

"Good?" Suzanne asked in a mumble as she chewed and swallowed her own sample.

"That was better—"

"Than you were expecting?"

"Yeah." Maddie nodded.

"I told you!" Suzanne grinned. "I'll make a sign for them and list the ingredients, and I bet we sell out of them by lunchtime."

"There." Suzanne held up a sign a couple of minutes later.

"We're selling them for a dollar fifty each?" Maddie asked.

"Yep. That way we make one dollar profit from each ball."

"They're pretty small," Maddie said doubtfully, "although delicious," she added. "Do you think people will buy them at that price?"

"You bet," Suzanne snapped her fingers. "But if we don't sell any by lunchtime, I guess we can give out some free samples." Her expression looked so sad that Maddie hoped their next customer would buy one.

"If I go now, I'll be back before the lunch rush." Maddie checked her watch.

"Go where? To interview the masseuse?"

"Yes."

Suzanne looked torn between wanting to accompany her and wanting to stay at the truck in case a pre-lunch customer wanted to buy a health ball.

"I'll stay here." Her gaze strayed to the healthy goodies she'd now placed on a plate covered with a plastic dome.

"Okay. I won't be long." Maddie paused. "Have you ever been there – to get a massage?"

"No," Suzanne replied. "I just happened to glance by one day when I was walking past and that's when I saw the narrow doorway with a sign saying there was a masseuse upstairs. But if I'd known he looked like that, I might have booked more than one by now." She winked.

Maddie suppressed a laugh. "I'll tell you what I find out."

"You better."

They both turned to look at Trixie, who still dozed on a stool.

"I'll look after her," Suzanne promised.

"Thanks." Maddie jumped out of the truck, her thoughts in a whirl. Looking at Trixie had jogged her memory; she had the tell the truth spell written on a piece of paper in her purse.

Should she use it on the masseuse?

She'd forgotten about it when their elderly first customer had stepped up to the counter. Perhaps because she was still recovering from getting up so early this morning?

Or maybe because she was worried something would go wrong if she tried to cast it?

Before she knew it, she'd arrived at the *"massage parlor"*. A discreet sign on the narrow glass door told her a masseuse was available upstairs.

Maddie walked up the wooden stairs, the sound of her work shoes on the steps alerting the masseuse that someone was arriving.

At the top of the landing, a wooden door with a metal plaque emblazoned with *Ramon – Qualified Masseuse* greeted her.

Maddie raised her hand. Should she knock? If someone was having a massage right now, she didn't want to interrupt.

Tap tap.

Just when she thought maybe she hadn't knocked hard enough, she heard a low male voice.

"Come in."

Inhaling deeply, Maddie pushed open the door and walked inside.

Cream walls and a small reception desk greeted her. Two comfortable looking chairs in the waiting room invited her to sit down.

A beaded curtain at the back of the tiny room signaled the treatment room.

"Can I help you?" The man sitting at the desk took her breath away.

Early forties, with jet black hair, liquid brown eyes framed with thick dark lashes, olive skin, and firm, sensual lips – he was exactly as their elderly customer had described.

Devilishly good looking.

There was a trace of a European accent in his voice, but Maddie couldn't place it right away.

"Hi." Her voice squeaked and she cursed silently.

"Hi." He smiled back at her.

Her insides began to melt. Had it really been so long since she'd had a date? *Focus.*

She reached into her purse and fingered the tell the truth spell.

"Um …" She attempted to gather her thoughts.

"You would like a massage?" he asked.

"Um …" *Yes please.* Her cheeks burned at the thought.

"My friend Linda – she said she came here," was the best Maddie could think up.

90

"Ah, Linda, yes. One of my favorite clients." His white teeth flashed in a gorgeous grin. At that very moment, Maddie couldn't blame Linda if she had strayed from her husband.

"She came here yesterday morning?" She cursed the up-speak in her voice.

"That's right." The man looked at her curiously. "I am Ramon. And you are?"

"Maddie." When he continued to look at her admiringly – was he flirting with her? – she added breathlessly, "I have a coffee truck in the town square."

"Ah, yes, I have seen it," he replied. "The only reason I have not visited is I prefer to make my own coffee. In Spain, we have a special technique to extract all the goodness from the beans. Here, in America, you have percolated coffee." He shuddered slightly.

"Not in my truck," Maddie stated. "I buy only the best beans and I attempt to bring out the flavors of each different roast."

"Then I must come by and try you one day," he said. "And then, perhaps you will sample me and my massages."

"Um … maybe," Maddie squeaked again. Wait until she told Suzanne! Knowing her friend and her adventurous side, Suzanne would probably book a massage right away.

"I have no clients now, if you would like to—" he waved toward the beaded curtain.

"I can't right now," Maddie said hurriedly. "I just thought I would talk to you first about what Linda gets—"

"You are romance writer too?"

"Yes," she blurted out before she could think better of it.

"Ah, that makes sense." He nodded. "You have a fire in your eyes and desire in your heart, no? Your smooth brown hair, your heart-shaped face, your amber eyes – you are what a heroine looks like."

Maddie had never thought of herself that way before, but she had to admit, it did have a flattering, poetic ring to it. But could he tell she was a witch? What he'd just described could loosely describe her witchy abilities – or the one she had, the ability to cast the coffee vision spell.

"But I did not think Linda told anyone about her secret yearning to become a romance writer." He frowned.

"We're in the same writers' group," Maddie fibbed, wondering at herself for jumping into a lie so quickly.

"Ah." His brow cleared. "What would you like to know? Although I must warn you that Linda paid me. I told her, "No, Linda, you must not," but she insisted. Said it was only fair. I booked her in as a client, and in the treatment room—" he gestured to the beaded curtain "—we talked about her hero, a young, handsome but impoverished Spaniard who was in love with the haughty Esmerelda and how he could win her heart."

"Goodness," Maddie said faintly.

"She did not tell you about her story?" he asked, his deep brown eyes studying over her.

"She said it was a secret, that she wasn't ready to share," Maddie dissembled.

"Linda was a private person." He nodded. "Unfortunately for me, she was still in love with her husband." His eyes smoldered. "She is a most beautiful woman."

"But isn't she older than you?" Maddie asked, thinking of her elderly customer's words only a couple of hours ago, that Linda was fifty-five.

"What is age?" He shrugged in a very European way. "If a woman is beautiful on the inside – and in this case on the outside as well – what do I care if she is older than me? I will still love her most completely and together we will share great passion." His voice dropped to a sexy growl.

"I'll think about it – about getting you to help with my novel, I mean," Maddie gabbled, taking a backward step.

"And I shall visit your coffee truck one day." He smiled, his eyes crinkling slightly at the corners, making him look even sexier.

"Oh-kay," she squeaked, waving her hand in a half wave before turning and pulling open the door.

Once outside on the landing, she fanned herself, then clomped down the stairs, not caring how much noise her shoes made.

Once she was outside on the street, the fresh air brushing against her face, she exhaled loudly.

Man. She'd been so flustered, she'd forgotten the words to the tell the truth spell and hadn't tested it out on him.

She didn't know if even Suzanne was ready for this – this – sex god. No wonder Linda had asked him for advice about her romance novel!

If that was the real reason she had gone there …

Or was Linda having an affair with Ramon, and the romance novel explanation was a cover?

There was only one way to find out.

CHAPTER 9

"Did you end up getting a massage?" Suzanne asked as Maddie returned to the truck.

Trixie stirred, lifting her head, as if wanting to hear Maddie's answer.

"No." Maddie shook her head. "But I did learn something interesting."

"What's that?"

Briefly, Maddie told her friend why Linda had gone to the massage parlor.

"But what if that's a story she and Ramon have cooked up together?" She fanned herself. "I don't even blame Linda if she is having an affair with him. The man is smoking hot, and I do mean smoking!"

"Wow, he must be something special if you're this affected by him." Suzanne viewed her thoughtfully. "Maybe I *should* book a massage with him."

"He might be too much even for you," Maddie warned.

"In that case, I'm definitely going to visit him." Suzanne giggled.

Maddie shook her head in mock disbelief, her gaze dropping to the tray of health balls, now almost half empty.

"How many balls did you sell?" she asked.

"Sixteen." Suzanne's eyes sparkled. "And the lunch rush is about to start." She nodded toward the crowd of people streaming into the park.

Maddie and Suzanne barely had a chance to talk for the next two hours as they were slammed with orders. To Suzanne's delight, the health balls sold out.

"We've made an extra forty dollars' profit!" Suzanne crowed once the last of the customers had departed.

They high-fived, then Maddie became serious.

"I think I should visit Linda and see if Ramon told the truth about her visits."

"Good idea. What if Joan found out and Linda killed her?"

"Do you think so?" There was skepticism in Maddie's voice.

"What if Joan threatened to go to Linda's husband and tell him?"

"Why would she do that?" Maddie frowned.

Suzanne shrugged. "Maybe they had a falling out. Maybe Linda was always cancelling their jogging sessions so she could visit Ramon instead, and Joan got fed up about it."

"We must never let that happen to us." Maddie touched Suzanne's arm.

"Promise." Suzanne smiled at her.

"Mrrow," Trixie agreed.

"Maybe I should come with you," Suzanne continued. "If Linda did kill Joan, then you shouldn't visit her alone."

"Good idea," Maddie said, a cold shiver running down her spine. "Trixie, we're going to visit someone."

The Persian hopped off the stool and padded over to the truck door, waiting to be let out.

"I'll put up a sign." Suzanne got out a piece of paper and a pen. "We should be back by 3.30, right?"

"Yep." Maddie nodded. "And then we better get started on the health balls for tomorrow."

"Mrrow."

***

"Maybe we should have contacted Detective Edgewater," Maddie whispered to Suzanne as they stood outside Linda's front door. Trixie waited for them in Maddie's car, her nose pressed to the open window, watching them.

"Too late now," Suzanne whispered back as the door slowly opened.

"Girls." Linda looked surprised to see them. "What brings you here?"

"I was thinking of getting a massage," Suzanne jumped in. "And I heard you go to Ramon in the town square."

Linda paled, her eyes widening. "You better come in."

They entered the house, decorated in shades of warm gray and cornflower blue.

Linda led them into a cozy kitchen, a counter with sturdy wooden stools dominating one half of the room.

"Please, sit," she indicated the stools.

Maddie and Suzanne hopped up onto a stool each.

"How did you find out about that?" Linda took a seat opposite them.

"Someone saw you go in there – yesterday morning," Maddie replied.

"Oh." Linda's face crumpled. "You have no idea how badly I feel about it. If I hadn't cancelled jogging with Joan to meet Ramon, maybe she would still be alive."

"Why did you go to see him?" Maddie asked, looking searchingly at Linda. She could see what Ramon had meant when he said Linda was a beautiful older woman. Her short dark hair was stylishly cut, her features had a timeless elegance about them, and her figure was slim.

Linda hesitated. "If you must know, he was helping me with research."

"Research?" Suzanne asked.

"Yes." The older woman flushed. "If I tell you, you have to promise not to tell anyone."

Maddie and Suzanne exchanged glances.

"We promise," they chorused.

"Well ... I'm writing a romance novel." Linda paused, but when they remained silent, she continued, "and one day I bumped into Ramon in the town square – literally bumped into him. He was so charming, and told me that he was a masseuse and where his shop was, that –

well – I thought it was the perfect opportunity to make my hero authentic, you know? My book is set in Spain and my hero is a poor, impetuous, handsome man, who pines for the beautiful but haughty Esmeralda, and—"

"It sounds interesting," Maddie said hastily. So far, Linda's story tallied with Ramon's.

"But why keep it a secret?" Suzanne asked curiously. "You're not doing anything wrong – are you?"

Maddie kicked Suzanne's calf.

"Ow." Suzanne rubbed her leg and frowned at her friend.

"No, we weren't – aren't – doing anything wrong." Linda looked guilty for a second. "Except … I don't really need to see Ramon for any more background. He's been a marvelous help, but … I can't stop myself going back to see him and talking to him about my novel. He's such a wonderful listener and – oh, girls, have you seen him? He's beautiful." She blushed.

Maddie found herself nodding in agreement.

"And not just on the outside, either. I enjoy being able to talk about my romance novel with someone. Nobody else knows about it – not even Joan knew. I have no idea if it has potential, but I enjoy writing about it and talking over the plot with Ramon. And maybe, someday, I can get it published." Pink spots of determination stood out on Linda's cheeks.

"What about your husband?" Suzanne asked, looking at Maddie as if wondering if it was safe to ask the question.

Maddie suddenly remembered the tell the truth spell. Now she wasn't flustered in a sexy European man's presence, would she be able to remember the incantation?

A calmness descended as she focused, and she felt like she did when she cast the coffee vision spell. Was it all her? Or was Trixie somehow lending her telepathic support from the car outside?

She could see the words in her mind. Silently, she uttered them, whispering, "Show me," at the end.

Luckily, neither Linda nor Suzanne seemed to notice her murmur.

Linda's gaze landed fondly on a silver-framed photo of herself and a tubby man of medium height with balding gray hair.

"I don't know if Fred would laugh at me," she said. "And if I told him about Ramon, he might be jealous, even though we're just friends."

Maddie nodded, knowing deep down that Linda told the truth. Was the spell working? Or her own intuition?

"So who would want to kill Joan?" Suzanne asked.

"I don't know." Linda shrugged. "As far as I know, she didn't have any enemies."

"Brian was thinking of retiring, right?" Maddie asked.

"Yes." Linda nodded her head. "But now ... I don't know. Continuing to work might help him through the grieving process."

"That's true," Maddie replied thoughtfully.

"You didn't notice any strangers hanging around lately?" Suzanne asked.

"No." Linda frowned in thought. "But I did notice the assistant librarian visiting Joan's house last week."

"Oh?" Maddie snapped her gaze to Linda's face.

"Yes. I believe it was last Tuesday. I only knew who she was because I've seen her when I've gone to the library. A pleasant girl, although I don't know her well. I thought it was a little strange, but she probably had library business to discuss with Brian."

Ever since Maddie had cast the truth spell, she knew that Linda had replied with total honesty to every question.

She racked her brains, but couldn't think of anything else to ask the older woman.

Suzanne must have felt the same, because she looked at Maddie and gave her the special eyebrow signal they had invented years ago, which meant, do you want to leave now?

"Thanks for talking to us." Maddie rose from her stool. "We are sorry about Joan," she said sincerely.

"Thank you," Linda replied. "And … you won't tell anyone about Ramon and my novel, will you?"

"Your secret is safe with us." Suzanne smiled. "Don't worry." She added, "As long as you give us a signed copy of your book when it's published."

"Deal." Linda's face relaxed into a smile.

Maddie and Suzanne left the house. Once the front door was shut behind them, Suzanne declared, "I am *definitely* visiting Ramon for a massage. The sooner the better."

Maddie laughed as they got into her car.

"Did you catch all that, Trixie?" she asked the cat, who hopped into her lap.

"Mrrow!"

"Did you help me cast the spell?" she whispered in the feline's ear.

A loud purr rumbled from the Persian's chest.

"What are you two talking about?" Suzanne asked.

Maddie told her about the truth spell as she started the ignition. Trixie hopped over to the rear seat, a satisfied look on her furry face.

"That's awesome, Mads!" Suzanne clicked her seatbelt into place. "Now you can do two spells."

"And we know that Linda is telling the truth – or at least she was for the second part of our questioning."

"That should help us," Suzanne said. "Where should we go next?"

"How about back to the coffee truck so we can start making more health balls?"

"And after that, we better visit Phoebe, the library assistant, again," Suzanne declared.

CHAPTER 10

Maddie and Suzanne took Trixie home, then hurried back to the coffee truck, made the health balls, locked up, and departed for the library.

"Phew!" Suzanne dramatically wiped her brow. "I am *definitely* going to relax in front of TV tonight."

"I know what you mean." Maddie yawned. "Don't forget, we got up earlier, too."

"Yeah. But it was worth it, wasn't it? We even had a couple of customers come back for more treats at lunchtime."

"It was a great idea of yours," Maddie admitted.

"Now all we have to do is keep up with demand!"

They arrived at the library.

"What are we going to ask her?" Suzanne turned to Maddie.

"What about Joan's husband's alibi? And why Phoebe visited him last week?"

"I'll sneak a peek and see if she's wearing her locket today," Suzanne added.

They walked into the library. Maddie scanned the space, looking for the library assistant. She stood at the far end of the room, putting books back on a shelf.

"Over there." Maddie nodded at the bookcase.

They trod lightly on the carpet, as if in silent agreement. *We don't want to spook her.*

Once they stood behind her, Maddie cleared her throat. She didn't want to give the woman a heart attack by startling her.

The library assistant whipped around.

"Can I help you?" She frowned, as if dimly recognizing them. "Oh, you came in yesterday, didn't you?"

"That's right, Phoebe," Maddie replied. "We're friends of Joan." The more she asked people questions, the closer she felt to Joan. It wasn't really a lie, she told herself.

Phoebe nodded as if remembering.

Today, she was dressed in a droopy black skirt and lavender blouse, trimmed with lace around the neckline. Dark circles under her eyes indicated she hadn't been sleeping well.

"We were wondering about the charity project Joan's husband told us about," Maddie said. "Is it still going ahead?"

"Oh – yes, I think so," Phoebe replied. "But maybe not as soon as Bri – Mr. Hodgeton hoped for. We might have to put it on hold for a while now because of what happened." She lowered her voice to a whisper.

"We understand," Suzanne said. "But …"

"Yes?" Phoebe looked around as if checking anyone else needed help, but apart from a couple of senior citizens dozing in armchairs, there weren't any other patrons.

"It sounds like it's a very big undertaking," Maddie put in smoothly, silently wondering at her new found confidence in asking potential suspects questions.

"Yes." The library assistant vigorously nodded her head. "It's going to be huge. There are so many children who go to school but are failing in literacy. Some of them can't even read simple words such as cat and mat." She sounded shocked.

"Brian and I are – were – going to work on it together."

"He came over to see you yesterday, didn't he?" Suzanne asked, peering intently at the other woman. "To talk about it?"

Library assistant suddenly looked flustered. "Why yes ... he did."

"That was the morning his wife was killed." Maddie didn't have to fake the sadness in her voice.

Library assistant looked discomfited. "Yes, that's right."

"And you went over to his house the week before, didn't you?" Suzanne blurted out.

"Yes, but – hey, why are you asking me all these questions?" Phoebe scowled at them. "The detective has already asked me about Mr. Hodgeton's whereabouts that day, and I told them. What has my visit to my boss's house got to do with anything?"

Maddie was taken aback by her sudden vehemence and since Suzanne was silent, she guessed her friend was too.

Phoebe drew herself up to her full height of five foot eight.

"For your information, I was at Mr. Hodgeton's house talking about the charity project. It's quite complex, and we don't have enough time to talk about it during work hours. Now, if you'll excuse me, I have work to do."

She wheeled the cart of books right past them, almost squashing their toes in the process.

"Wow," Suzanne breathed once she'd departed. "Do you think we hit a nerve?"

"Definitely," Maddie said. "Something we said certainly made her jumpy."

"We just have to work out what it was."

***

"Shoot. I forgot to cast the truth spell," Maddie grumbled as they made their way back to the truck. She kept her voice low so the occasional passerby wouldn't hear.

"I'm sure she wasn't telling the truth about *something*," Suzanne remarked. "It's a shame Trixie wasn't with us – maybe she could have sensed what was up with that woman."

"Yeah." Maddie smiled at the thought of her pretty cat strolling into the library with them. "I wonder if they have a no cats policy?"

"Hey, is there an invisibility spell in your book?" Suzanne asked as they unlocked the coffee truck. "Maybe you could make Trixie invisible, and she could accompany us everywhere, no problem."

"I don't think there is." Maddie wrinkled her brow as she thought about the spells she'd studied in the ancient tome. "But if there is, I wouldn't be able to see where she goes," Maddie pointed out. "What if she got bored and wandered off?"

"She'd probably know exactly how to find you," Suzanne said as she checked on the trays of health balls they'd made thirty minutes ago. "Just like she did the first time she walked into the coffee shop, and made you instantly fall in love with her."

"Who wouldn't?" Maddie smiled as she thought about Trixie.

Suzanne sighed. "I wish I was a witch like you. You're so lucky, Mads."

"Do you think so?" Maddie wrinkled her nose. "I can only do two spells, and

I've been so shaken with what's happened to Joan that I haven't had that little feeling again that tells me when to cast the coffee vision spell."

"It will come back." Suzanne touched Maddie's arm. "I'm sure of it."

"Maybe you should be the witch instead of me," Maddie joked, knowing deep down that if she did lose her powers, she would feel like she'd lost part of herself, even if she could only cast two spells. And what about Trixie? Would the loveable cat stay with her if she was no longer a witch? Or would she find another mistress – one with full magical powers?

"Hey, maybe there's a spell in your book about turning someone into a witch!" Suzanne grinned. "Then we could both be witches."

"I'll have a look tonight," Maddie promised, although she didn't remember seeing such a spell in the book. Could you really turn someone into a witch just like that? Or was it part of your DNA before you were even born?

"Call me and tell me if you find anything like that in the book," Suzanne said.

"I will." Maddie jumped into the driver's seat and turned on the ignition. "Let's go home."

Once they arrived at Maddie's house, Suzanne turned to her. "Hey, I forgot to tell you I had a good look at Phoebe's blouse when we were at the library and I could definitely see a gold chain around her neck. But if it was the locket, it was tucked into her blouse."

Hmm." Maddie turned off the engine, the last chug dying away. "That's interesting. Don't you think it's a bit weird she went over to his house last week to talk about this charity project? And that Brian went over to her house yesterday morning to talk about it again? It must be a huge enterprise if it requires them to talk about it out of work hours twice."

"And it was quiet in the library just now," Suzanne said thoughtfully. "She seemed to be the only employee there and didn't appear to have a problem handling the workload."

"So why wouldn't they have time to talk about the charity project when they're both working?" Maddie finished her friend's thought.

"Unless it gets busy at times," Suzanne offered. "Maybe they have a toddler's story time or something during the day."

"But if she's innocent, why would she get angry about us asking her those questions?" Maddie started up the porch steps. "It just seemed out of proportion."

"I know what you mean." Suzanne snapped her fingers. "What if she does have the hots for Brian – her boss?"

"And she killed Joan to get her out of the way." Maddie unlocked her front door. Trixie was nowhere in sight.

"Because Phoebe and Brian were having an affair!" Suzanne followed her inside.

Maddie faced her friend, nodding in agreement. "I think that makes sense. Brian's initials are on her locket, and she got all flustered about that locket last time. She's visited his house, and he's visited hers. Do you really think he was being unfaithful to Joan?"

"There's only one way to find out."

CHAPTER 11

As Maddie and Suzanne entered the living room, Trixie hopped off the couch and trotted to greet them.

"Hi, Trixie." Suzanne bent and stroked the Persian's shoulder.

"Mrrow!" Trixie turned to Maddie, looking at her expectantly.

Maddie crouched down, and rubbed the Persian behind the ear. Instantly, a loud purr filled the room.

"Hey, we could look at the book now." Suzanne's gaze strayed to the sofa, where the witchcraft book lay.

"Okay." Maddie sat down on the couch. Trixie joined her, sitting on the soft, periwinkle sofa cushions. Suzanne sat on the other side of the book.

Maddie turned the pages, starting from the beginning, but didn't see anything about turning someone into a witch. There were spells for sleeping soundly, glamour spells, love spells, and even instructions on how to make yourself disappear for a few seconds, but nothing about how to gain witchy powers.

"That disappearing spell sounds cool. It's *almost* like an invisibility spell." Suzanne's eyes sparkled. "Just imagine what kind of sleuthing you could do if you could make yourself disappear for a short time."

"Mmm." Maddie didn't sound convinced. "But what if I couldn't make myself reappear? What if remained invisible?"

"Does it say you can make someone else invisible? Or does it have to be yourself?"

Maddie scanned the wording. "Just myself."

"Oh." Suzanne sounded disappointed.

"But this way, at least you'll be visible when you go to visit Ramon," Maddie teased.

"There is that." Suzanne giggled.

After talking about everything they'd discovered that day, Suzanne departed, giving Trixie a goodbye pat. Now they'd already made the health balls for the next day, they didn't have to get up early tomorrow.

Once Suzanne left the house, Maddie sat on the sofa with Trixie, watching a crime show on TV. But she couldn't concentrate – all she could think of was: did Phoebe, the library assistant, kill Joan?

***

Just as Maddie and Suzanne opened up for business the next day, their first customer was Brian, Joan's husband.

"Hi, Mr. Hodge – Brian." Maddie greeted him, a little surprised at his presence.

"Hi." He smiled briefly. "I thought I'd try the coffee Joan raves – raved – about." His smile dimmed.

"Of course. What would you like?"

"How about a latte?" He pulled out his wallet.

"It's on the house," Maddie said hurriedly, as she busied herself at the coffee machine. Hissing and grinding ensued. His request for the same drink that Joan used to order made her shiver. Did he know that was his wife's regular drink? Or did he usually drink spiced lattes as well?

"Hi Brian," Suzanne greeted the man, only a little surprise in her tone.

"Hi." Brian nodded at her.

"Would you like to try a health ball?" Suzanne showed him the tray full of coconut cacao balls they'd made yesterday. "On the house."

"Thanks." He helped himself to a round morsel, and began chewing. "That was good."

"Thank you." Suzanne smiled at him. "It's our new line. I don't think anyone else around here sells them."

"Here's your latte." Maddie pushed the cardboard cup across the counter. "I hope you enjoy it."

Brian took a sip, satisfaction crossing his face. "Now that's what I call a good coffee."

"We like to think so," Suzanne said, grinning. "Maddie makes the best coffee in town."

"Now I know why Joan kept badgering me to come here and try it myself."

"How is everything going?" Maddie asked. Joan's husband appearing like this would save her and Suzanne a visit to him later. Before Suzanne left Maddie's house last night, they'd discussed interviewing him today to try to get to the bottom of

119

whether he was having an affair with his library assistant.

"The funeral is going to be held in a couple of days' time." He looked sorrowful. "Once Joan's body is released." His voice cracked.

"Will you be going back to work after – after everything?" Suzanne put in. "Or will you be having more time off?"

"I think it's best if I go back to the library as soon as possible," he replied.

"We were at the library yesterday," Maddie said tentatively. "Phoebe, the library assistant, seems very capable."

"She's a great employee." Brian nodded. "She'll probably have my job one day."

"That charity project you're planning with her is still going ahead, right?" Suzanne asked.

"I hope so." He took another sip of coffee.

"It must be a big undertaking if you meet outside work to discuss it," Maddie said innocently. When he frowned, she continued, a knot of tension in her stomach, "Someone mentioned Phoebe visited your house last week."

He looked puzzled for a split-second. "Oh, yeah." His brow cleared. "That's right." He took a big swallow of coffee. Thanks for the coffee." He lifted the cup in salute. "I've got to be going now. Get an early jump on the day."

He walked across the town square. As soon as he was out of sight, another customer stepped up to the counter.

"Hello, girls." Detective Edgewater greeted them.

"Hi." Suzanne grabbed the plate of health balls and held it out in front of him. "Would you like one?"

"What are they?" He looked at the morsels doubtfully.

"Full of goodness," Suzanne enthused. "Come on, detective, you liked Maddie's coffee, didn't you? So far everyone who's tried one of these has raved about it."

Maddie didn't know if that was strictly true, but they hadn't received any complaints. *And,* they had experienced repeat customers coming back for more of the healthy bites.

"The ingredients are listed here." Maddie pointed to the list Suzanne had made yesterday and placed in front of the domed plate.

Detective studied the list. "Hmm. Okay. Give me one. And that coffee you made me before."

"Sure thing, sir." Maddie busied herself with the coffee machine, the sounds of grinding and whirring filling the air. Pleasure bubbled through her as she worked; she'd converted a new customer to her coffee.

The detective tasted the health ball, an expression of pleased surprise crossing his face.

"Not bad, girls. Not bad."

"Thanks." Suzanne smiled. "Would you like another?"

"Why not?" he shrugged. "I didn't have time for breakfast today."

"That will be seven dollars and forty cents, please." Suzanne held out her hand for the money.

He blinked. "No wonder you girls make a living at this." He pulled a ten-dollar bill from his wallet. "I might need to get a second job if this becomes a habit," he joked.

"And it would be totally worth it." Suzanne handed him his change and the second health ball.

The detective munched, then swallowed. "But your coffee isn't the only reason I'm here," he said. "Why was Mr. Hodgeton here just now?"

"I don't know." Maddie looked as surprised as she felt at the question. "He said he wanted to try my coffee – apparently Joan told him how good it was."

"Hmm." The detective took a sip of the vanilla cappuccino Maddie pushed across the counter to him. "Well, I wanted to warn you girls not to interfere with the case. I know you visited the library yesterday."

"What's wrong with going to the library?" Suzanne asked innocently.

Maddie darted a glance at her friend, Suzanne's tone arousing her suspicions.

"Nothing – if the only reason you went there was to borrow a book," the detective said sternly.

"How did you know we went to the library?" Maddie asked, furrowing her brow.

"People talk." He wagged a finger at them. "Do you think I'm not going to speak to everyone connected with the case? I talked to the library assistant yesterday, apparently just after you left there. Of course she was going to tell me about you two interrogating her."

"Of course." Suzanne made a sour face.

"It wasn't really interrogating," Maddie put in.

"Whatever it was, you two need to stop." He took another sip of his drink. "Stick to making fancy coffee drinks and those balls, whatever they're called. Otherwise, you might be drinking percolated coffee down at the station."

He departed, striding across the green.

"I think that proves my theory," Maddie said slowly. "Why would Phoebe, the library assistant, complain to him about us if she isn't guilty?"

"Exactly!" Suzanne shook her water bottle. "I thought she was guilty yesterday and now I'm even more convinced."

Before Maddie could reply, a wave of customers stood in front of the truck, pulling out their wallets.

"We'll talk about this later," Maddie whispered, before turning to the first customer.

One hour later, when there were only a couple of people left to serve, Suzanne flopped onto a stool.

"Wow!" She took a sip of water. "That was insane."

"Tell me about it," Maddie agreed.

"Hello, girls." The senior citizen with the pink rinse in her hair, who'd visited the truck yesterday, stepped up to the counter. "Can you give me the same coffee I had yesterday, dear?"

"Of course." Luckily, Maddie usually remembered her customers' orders if they were regulars or even semi-regulars – unless they were slammed with a crowd demanding coffee right away and she didn't have time to look up to see who she was making each drink for.

"You had a cappuccino, right?" Maddie smiled at the senior, the machine already grinding and hissing.

"That's right, dear." The elderly woman rifled through her black purse for her wallet. "Here you go." She handed a bill to Suzanne.

"How about a delicious, healthy treat?" Suzanne held out the plastic domed plate to the woman. "They're selling like hotcakes!"

The senior wrinkled her nose as she looked at the coconut covered balls. "I don't think so, dear. All that shredded coconut might play havoc with my dentures."

"Oh." Suzanne's expression dropped.

"But I'll be sure to tell my friends about them," the senior continued. "Why, I'm sure Joan's husband would enjoy them." She tsked. "I don't know what he's going to do now for meals. He isn't much of a cook."

"He tried one this morning." Suzanne smiled at the elderly woman.

"He might become of your regulars, then." The senior beamed at both of them as Maddie handed over the cappuccino.

An alarm pinged in Maddie's brain. While she'd been making the coffee, she'd listened to the conversation as well. It was something the elderly customer had just said that had given her a jolt of – something. Intuition? Half remembering

126

what someone had told her during the last two days? What was it?

"Thank you, girls." The senior strolled across the square, taking tiny sips of coffee as she went.

"Another satisfied customer," Suzanne said, counting the treats remaining on the plate. "But not a health ball fan."

"Maybe you could come up with a recipe without coconut," Maddie suggested. "Easy to chew and swallow ingredients that don't get stuck in false teeth, and you could call it Goodies for Seniors." As Suzanne stared at her, she added, "Or something like that."

"That's brilliant!" Suzanne grinned. "I'll get started on it right away."

"As long as I don't have to get up early again," Maddie joked.

"Don't worry, Mads, I can do it during our slow periods – now that we've been warned off from sleuthing."

"I know." Maddie frowned. "Surely it's obvious to the detective that Phoebe the library assistant killed Joan?"

"Maybe we should march into the station and tell him," Suzanne suggested. "And bring a few health balls as well. We might convert the staff in there and get more customers."

"Or bribe our way out of jail with them," Maddie teased. Then she sobered. "But what are we going to do, Suze? Why hasn't he arrested Phoebe yet?"

"We don't know that he hasn't," Suzanne said slowly. "Do we?"

They stared at each other, their eyes widening.

***

But when they visited the library later that day, with the excuse that they were actually going to borrow some books – Suzanne grabbing the first book off the first shelf she passed, which turned out to be a men's health book – Phoebe worked the desk, helping a thirty-something blonde check out a racy romance.

"Grr," Suzanne growled. "What is wrong with that detective?"

Before Maddie could answer, the library assistant looked up, blanching when she saw them.

"What are you two doing here?" she demanded in an angry whisper.

"Borrowing a book." Suzanne waved the book in the air, then placed it on the desk.

"Fine." Phoebe snatched Suzanne's library card, scanned it, and then did the same with the book, a beep emitting. "Here you go." Her eyebrows rose as she noticed the subject of the book.

"Thanks." Suzanne tucked the hardback under her arm.

Maddie sketched a wave at the library assistant as she and Suzanne walked out of the building.

"What are you going to do with that book?" Maddie asked as they headed back to the coffee truck. By now it was after four - they'd closed up the truck before going to the library.

Suzanne shrugged. "Maybe I'll give it to my brother to read." She flicked through the pages. "Ooh – it's got a chapter on sex. Maybe I'll read that first."

"You're naughty!" Maddie shook her head, smiling.

"That's why you like me." Suzanne grinned.

"But," Maddie sobered, "our library visit didn't clear anything up. If Phoebe hasn't been arrested yet, does that mean she's innocent? And if so, then who is the killer?"

CHAPTER 12

When Maddie arrived home, she checked the mailbox. Only one unaddressed white envelope. She frowned. That was strange. She took it out and carried it inside with her.

"Hey, Trixie," she greeted the cat. The Persian was curled up on the sofa, next to *Wytchcraft for the Chosen*.

"Mrrow." Trixie looked at the envelope expectantly.

"I wonder what it is." The envelope wasn't sealed – the triangular flap was just folded inside the bottom half. Maddie pulled out a piece of paper, the words scrawled in big black ink.

STOP SNOOPING.

Maddie stared at the piece of paper, then flung it away from her, as if it were a snake attempting to bite her. She sank down on the sofa.

Trixie jumped into her lap.

"Who would send such a thing?" Maddie whispered, stroking her cat with a trembling hand.

The killer. Obviously the killer had found out she and Suzanne had been asking questions – *or the killer was someone they'd already spoken to.* Like Phoebe, the library assistant. Maddie still didn't know why that woman hadn't been arrested. All the signs seemed to point to her as the murderer.

She reached for the phone and speed-dialed.

"Can you come over? I've got something to show you."

***

"There's no way Detective Edgewater would send this to you," Suzanne said, turning the piece of plain white note paper over in her hands. She'd arrived a few minutes after Maddie had called her,

"I agree. He'd probably arrest us instead." Maddie's voice was gloomy.

"Mrrow!" Trixie agreed.

"Do you know what this means, Mads?" Suzanne's eyes lit up with excitement. "You're getting close to finding out who the killer is!"

"Do you think so?" Maddie asked, a hint of skepticism in her voice. "I thought for sure it was Phoebe, the library assistant, but she hasn't been arrested. So maybe the detective doesn't think it's her."

"Or maybe he's giving her just enough rope to hang herself with," Suzanne said thoughtfully. She waved the note in the air. "You should show him this."

"So he can lecture us again?" Maddie wrinkled her nose. "And it's got our fingerprints on it now. Even if whoever wrote the note wore gloves, it's probably been handled too much by us to pick up a trace of anything, like DNA, from the writer."

"I still think you should show him," Suzanne insisted.

"Okay," Maddie sighed. "As soon as the morning rush is over tomorrow, I'll go down to the station. I just hope he doesn't arrest *me*."

***

Maddie sighed as she left the coffee truck the next morning and began walking to the sheriff's department, a couple of blocks from the town square.

What was the point of being a witch – or supposedly a witch – if her limited powers weren't helping her discover who the murderer was?

She hadn't had another opportunity to try out the tell the truth spell, either. Or had the urge to cast the other spell she could do, the coffee vision spell.

Perhaps Suzanne was right – all her powers would arrive after the next full moon – or maybe this was the extent of her powers – the ability to cast two spells correctly.

She took a deep breath as she opened the glass door to the sheriff's department. Suzanne was back at the coffee truck, serving any customers they had during their slow period. Although the coffee machine was Maddie's domain, Suzanne handled the register, made the tea, and grabbed the bottled water for customers. But she also knew how to make a pretty good coffee – maybe not as great as Maddie's, but far superior to the swill the local coffee shop served. And now,

Suzanne was in charge of producing the health balls, too.

Just as Maddie was going to ask for Detective Edgewater at the front desk, he emerged from a short hallway, looking surprised to see her.

"Miss Goodwell."

"Hi, Detective Edgewater." The warning note she'd received seemed to burn a hole in the purse slung over her shoulder. "Do you have a minute?"

"Sure." He checked his scratched silver watch. "Let's go in here." He steered her into a small, drab room off the hallway.

"What can I do for you?" He remained standing until she sat down on an uncomfortable black plastic chair.

"I received a note yesterday in my mailbox." Maddie put her purse on the gray metal table and dug out the envelope. "Here." She pushed it across the table.

He frowned, then pulled out a pair of blue latex gloves from his pocket. After putting them on, he carefully plucked out the note from the white envelope.

"Well, well," he said softly, his eyes focusing on her face. "I told you two not to interfere, didn't I?"

135

"Yes, sir," Maddie replied, feeling like she was in the principal's office in grade school – although that had never happened.

"Did your friend Suzanne receive one too?"

"No." Maddie shook her head.

"I suppose she touched it as well as you?"

"Yes." Maddie swallowed under his intent gaze. "After I saw what it was, I called Suzanne and she came over, and I showed it to her."

"Have you shown it to anyone else?"

"No."

"Was the envelope sealed?"

"No, sir. It was just like that, the flap tucked inside the bottom half of the envelope."

"Okay." He gingerly put the note back into the envelope. "I'll send this to the lab for analysis, but it will probably take a while for them to come up with anything. They're backed up at the moment. And when they do check it out, they probably won't find much. The writer likely wore gloves, and since the envelope was unsealed, there won't be any DNA they can pick up from saliva."

Maddie zipped up her purse, the rasp echoing in the sudden quiet of the room.

He wagged a finger at her. "I'm sorry you received this, but maybe now you and your friend realize how serious a murder investigation is. Don't go around asking questions about anyone. Don't go to the library unless you have genuine business there. And by business, I mean borrowing or returning library books. Nothing else. Understand?"

"Yes, sir." Maddie saw the stern expression on his face. He meant what he said.

"Otherwise, I'll have to bring you down here and think about charging you for interfering in an official investigation."

Maddie swallowed hard. She definitely didn't want *that* to happen.

"I understand."

"Good." He rose, and she did the same. "Go back to your truck and keep making coffee and those ball things. Concentrate on that."

She nodded, feeling a little patronized. Had he noticed that the library assistant wore a gold locket around her neck with the same initials as Joan's husband? Did he know that Linda, Joan's neighbor and best friend, had visited Ramon, the sexy Spanish masseuse the morning Joan was murdered, instead of staying home because she'd been "unwell"?

She mentally shrugged. He could find out those pieces of information on his own.

Maddie left the station, deep in thought. Some of her indignation had faded. She knew Detective Edgewater was correct; she and Suzanne should leave the sleuthing to the professionals, but still …

What was the point of having the ability to cast the coffee vision spell if she was unable to get justice for Joan?

When she reached the coffee truck, Suzanne looked at her eagerly. "Well? What did Detective Edgewater say?"

"Not to interfere." Maddie hopped into the truck. There were no customers around, so she could talk freely. Trixie had decided to stay home that day. "Or else I might be charged with interfering in an investigation."

Suzanne scowled. "After all the info we've found out! Did you tell him about the locket on the library assistant's neck?"

"No."

"Why not?"

"There wasn't an opportunity." How could she tell her friend how chastised she'd felt at the station, with the detective lecturing her? And, he had a point.

"Maybe he's right," Maddie continued. "I definitely don't want to be arrested. And—" she looked at Suzanne "— receiving that note did shake me up a bit. Maybe it's best for all of us, including Trixie, that we back off. Concentrate on making senior citizen friendly health balls."

Suzanne waved a hand in the air. "Already done that. I've come up with a recipe I think will work and this afternoon I'll go and buy the ingredients."

"See?" Maddie arched an eyebrow at her friend. "Who needs to add sleuthing to our lives when we've got all this?" She gestured to the coffee machine and the interior of the truck.

"And Trixie." Suzanne grinned.

"And Trixie."

CHAPTER 13

For the next couple of days, Maddie, Suzanne, and Trixie concentrated on their real business – their coffee truck. Well, Maddie and Suzanne did, anyway. Trixie joined them for one day, then the next decided to stay at home, guarding the spell book as if she were worried someone would come in and steal it.

"When is the full moon, anyway?" Maddie asked on the third morning after handing in the *STOP SNOOPING* note to Detective Edgewater.

"Next week." Suzanne looked excited. "Then we'll find out if you've attained your full powers."

They'd just finished serving the mid-morning crowd. The senior citizen health balls had been a big success with their elderly customers, and now Maddie as well as Suzanne was interested in finding new recipes for these healthy treats, so their clientele wouldn't get bored with seeing the same goodies available every day.

Maddie made herself and Suzanne a mocha, and sat on the stool, swinging her feet in the air. "I thought I'd go to the library while it's quiet." She gestured to the front counter. Not a soul in sight.

"Sure," Suzanne agreed. "I can handle things here. But didn't the detective warn us off the library?"

"Only if we had non-genuine business." Maddie took a sip of her coffee. "And this is totally legit. I want to check out some healthy cook books. Now you've got me interested in creating new recipes for our customers."

"Awesome!" Suzanne grinned. "I told you the health balls would be a big hit."

"And you were right." Maddie returned her smile. "And I bet Claudine isn't very happy about it, either."

"Ha ha!" Suzanne crowed. "Funny how she hasn't visited the truck again, isn't it?"

They exchanged knowing looks. Claudine hadn't made the café a pleasant place to work in, and having her coffee truck business do so well gave Maddie an extra glow of satisfaction.

Maddie drained her cup and stood. "I won't be long."

"Okay." Suzanne waved goodbye, before sipping at her mocha.

During the short walk to the library, Maddie thought about different flavor combinations they could try with the health balls. Maybe lemon, or strawberry. Definitely a deep, rich chocolate – without dates. But would that still make it healthy? Wouldn't it be more like a truffle? Perhaps she could suggest to Suzanne they make truffles as well, for people who wanted to indulge in something totally *unhealthy*.

She entered the library. The room was quiet: no patrons browsing the shelves, whispering to each other, or dozing in armchairs.

Walking over to the first bookcase, she scanned the non-fiction listing. Cookbooks should be in the 641 number range a couple of bookcases away.

Maddie found the recipe books, skimming the titles, looking for ones on healthy eating. Would a no sugar cookbook be helpful? Although, she didn't know how anyone could go through life without at least a little sugar in their day.

The sound of a book being placed on a shelf nearby made her pause. She'd thought she was all alone in the library. She hadn't even seen Phoebe, the library assistant, or Joan's husband Brian at the desk. Maybe whoever was on duty had to go to the bathroom and had just come back and was now shelving books.

She peered through the open part of the bookcase. Joan's husband was opposite. On her way to the cookbook shelves, she'd noticed that that particular section started on the opposite end of the two-sided bookcase, and wrapped around to her side. She'd had a quick look at those books first, but they'd seemed like general cookbooks, including recipes for beginners.

Should she say hello to Joan's husband? Call out quietly through the bookcase? Before she could make up her mind, she watched him pluck a book from the shelf. A cookbook for beginners! But why was he taking it from the shelf? Shouldn't he be placing it there if he was putting books away?

She watched him walk to the librarian's desk and scan the book. A soft beep emitted. Then she saw him place it under the desk.

What was he doing?

Why was he checking out a beginner's cookbook? Was he borrowing it for himself?

She froze as fragments of conversation zoomed through her brain. Brian had told her and Suzanne that he'd gone home the morning Joan had died to get some meat out of the freezer to defrost because it was his turn to cook that night.

Their elderly customer with pink hair who had told them about Linda visiting Ramon, the sexy masseuse, mentioned later that Brian wasn't much of a cook.

And now that Joan, his wife, was dead, he was borrowing a beginner's cookbook.

If he couldn't cook, why was he going to make dinner that night? Beef bourgignon, no less.

Unless …

Maddie's fingers trembled as she clutched the no sugar recipe book to her chest. Should she? She glanced around. The library seemed to be deserted apart from her and Brian.

Taking a deep breath, she walked over to the desk, placing her book before him.

"Hello Brian," she said as calmly as she could.

"Hello, Maddie." He glanced at the title before scanning it. A soft beep filled the room. "Into healthy eating?"

"Something like that." She took the book from him. "What about you?"

He shrugged. "I like a decent meal. If that means it's got some sugar and fat in it, all the better."

"It must be hard being on your own," Maddie said, hoping there wasn't a tremor in her voice. "Joan did all the cooking, didn't she?"

"Yes—" He stilled as he seemed to realize what he'd just admitted. His gaze darkened, zeroing in on her.

"I saw you borrow that beginner cookbook just now," she told him, drawing herself up as tall as she could, hoping he didn't realize her knees were trembling. This was the moment she needed her witchy powers, if she had any, if only to give her added confidence.

"I hoped my note would scare you off," he snarled, his face twisting. Gone was the mild-mannered head librarian and in his place was a murderer. "My mistake."

"Actually, your mistake was claiming to cook when you can't," Maddie informed him. "Someone told me you weren't much of a chef, but it wasn't until now when I saw you with that recipe book that all the pieces came together. You didn't return home that day to get the meat out of the freezer for dinner, did you?"

"No," he growled. "I came home so I could discover my wife, lying dead on the kitchen floor. It was a pretty clever idea."

"So where were you earlier that morning?"

"He was with me, just like he told the detective." Phoebe, the library assistant, entered the room from the back hallway. She stood by his side and took his hand. "I don't know what you're insinuating, but it isn't true!"

Maddie stared at Phoebe, that woman's face shining with devotion as she looked at Brian. Was Maddie wrong? Was Brian actually innocent?

No.

"But I bet the time you arrived at Phoebe's apartment was later than the time you told the detective," Maddie said slowly. "Because you had to kill Joan

147

before you drove over to Phoebe's apartment."

"Aren't you the clever one," he sneered.

"Brian?" Phoebe whispered, tugging on his hand. "What's she saying isn't true – is it?"

"Yeah." He shrugged.

"So that's why you asked me to lie to Detective Edgewater and tell him you arrived fifteen minutes earlier than you actually did? You said you were innocent and if I didn't help you with your alibi, they'd arrest you!" Phoebe stared at him in horror, dropping his hand.

"Phoebe, it wasn't my fault. Joan pushed me too far. And you were partly to blame." He scowled at his employee. "She told me that morning while she waved divorce papers in my face that you'd visited her the previous week. Telling her that we were in love and she should give me up so you could marry me." He shook his head in disgust. "She actually decided to follow your advice. Said she was sick of my flirting with other women over the years. That you were welcome to me."

He shook Phoebe's shoulders. "I couldn't have that. You know I've been planning to retire early. How do you think I could afford to do that if it wasn't for Joan's money?"

Phoebe stared at him, her mouth parted.

"Yeah, you didn't know about that, did you? Joan had a small private income, which meant we could live comfortably on our combined money, and she'd finally agreed that I could retire *now*. But after your visit to her, she changed her mind."

"But Brian, I thought we were *in love*." Phoebe's face crumpled, and she swayed.

"In love?" He snorted. "No. We enjoyed a mild flirtation, that's all. God knows, there was no one else to amuse myself with in this place – unless I wanted to dally with fat Carol, the Wednesday volunteer."

Maddie took a step back, hoping they wouldn't notice. She had to tell Suzanne right away, as well as Detective Edgewater, what was going on. Her hand slid into her open purse, her fingers finding the buttons on her cell phone. Silently speed-dialing Suzanne, she hoped Brian and Phoebe were so wrapped up in their conversation that they wouldn't notice her stealthy move.

"I had your initials engraved on my locket!" Phoebe wailed, pulling out the gold necklace from underneath her blouse and ripping it from her neck. She flung it at him. "How could you do this to me?"

"You're a fantasist," he said dismissively. "How could you think I was in love with you? You'd look okay if you smarted yourself up a bit, wore makeup, and sprayed some perfume on yourself, but right now you're not exactly any man's dream."

"Why, you—" Phoebe's fingers turned into claws as she lunged at him.

"Stop it!" Maddie's voice held unexpected power as she vaulted over the desk and dragged the other woman off Brian.

"But ... but ..." Phoebe panted with fury, struggling in Maddie's surprisingly strong grip. "Let me at him! He deserves it!"

"I know," Maddie agreed. "But let the sheriff's department handle it."

"Too late," Brian jeered, reaching under the desk and drawing out a gun.

"You two are the only ones who know I murdered Joan. Once I take care of you, I'll have plenty of time to make my getaway."

"I wouldn't count on it." Suzanne appeared in the library entrance, glaring at Brian.

"Me either." Detective Edgewater flanked Suzanne, holding his own gun in his right hand. "Drop it right now. Backup is on its way."

Brian glowered at the detective and Suzanne, before turning his attention back to Maddie and Phoebe. The gun wavered in his hand, as if he couldn't make up his mind what to do. Then, with a loud groan, he slowly lowered his arm, the gun dangling in his hand.

"Place it on the ground *now.*" The detective barked. "And step away."

Brian obeyed.

"Placed your hands on your head."

Scowling, Brian followed the order.

"Maddie and Phoebe, come over here," Detective Edgewater directed.

Maddie and Phoebe did so, the library assistant sobbing as if her heart had broken.

Once the detective had cuffed Brian and called the station, he frowned at Maddie and Suzanne.

"Didn't I tell you girls to stop interfering?"

"I wasn't," Maddie protested. "Not since I handed in the note to you at the station. I was looking for healthy cook books and I saw Brian with a beginner's cook book and everything just fell into place."

"We had Brian on our radar," the detective growled. "If it hadn't been for you calling your friend and leaving the line open, we wouldn't have known you were in trouble. I was going to visit Brian later today, but by then it would have been too late – for both of you."

"Are you okay?" Suzanne hugged Maddie.

"I guess." She returned the hug, relieved that it was all over. But why were her knees suddenly wobbly now she wasn't in danger?

"Let's go back to the truck." Suzanne put an arm around Maddie's shoulders. "I think you definitely need a coffee."

"Yes," Maddie agreed. "Definitely."

***

When they returned to the truck, Suzanne fussed over Maddie, ordering her to sit down while she made the coffee for a change.

After Maddie's first sip of a cappuccino, her knees stopped shaking.

"Ah, that's better." She smiled at Suzanne.

"You need a health ball." Suzanne pressed one into her friend's hand.

Maddie nodded, chewing on the soft chocolatey tasting treat.

"You gave me one for old people?"

Suzanne grinned. "I figured that was all you could handle right now."

"I think you're right." Maddie sipped her coffee. "Thank goodness you heard what was going on over my cell phone. I was worried you wouldn't be able to hear Brian talking since the phone was in my purse. But I didn't know what else to do."

"I was just about to head over to the library to see what was keeping you," Suzanne said, flopping onto the second stool and taking a swallow of her own

153

coffee. "Then I got your call, and at the same time, Detective Edgewater arrived for—" she smiled briefly "—a vanilla cappuccino and a health ball."

"Lucky," Maddie said wholeheartedly.

"Yeah." Suzanne nodded. "He warned me to stay here, but I wasn't going to let you face a murderer on your own." She touched Maddie's arm. "We're a team."

"The three of us." Maddie got out her cell phone and pressed a button. "Look, Trixie is still guarding the spell book, but it's open." She stared at the image on her phone. "The book was definitely closed when I left this morning."

"Maybe she was helping in some way?" Suzanne offered. "Maybe she was looking up a spell to assist you?"

Maddie stared at her friend.

"Hey, don't look at me like that," Suzanne protested. "I don't think it's that crazy of an idea."

"Not crazy at all," Maddie said slowly. "You hadn't arrived yet, but Phoebe tried to attack Brian when she found out he wasn't in love with her, and somehow, my voice sounded totally confident when I yelled at them to stop it *and* I vaulted over the desk and pulled her off him."

"I didn't know you were that athletic." Suzanne looked at her admiringly.

"I'm not. That's the point. It sort of felt like when I cast the coffee vision spell. And now—" Maddie pointed to her phone, Trixie still hunched over the open spell book, "—the book is open. What if Trixie was able to somehow help me?"

"Giving you a dose of witchy power?" Suzanne asked.

"Exactly."

"She is so totally your familiar." Suzanne smiled.

"Totally." Maddie grinned.

***

Just as Maddie and Suzanne were packing up for the day, Detective Edgewater knocked on the truck window.

"Hi, sir," Maddie greeted him, wondering if he was going to chastise her once more.

"Miss Goodwell." He nodded. "I'm glad you're okay."

"Me too," Maddie replied with feeling.

155

"I just wanted to give you an update. Brian has confessed in a formal statement. Apparently he killed his wife because she was threatening to divorce him, and that would mean he couldn't take early retirement." He tsked. "He says he just lost it. And he was the person who sent you the threatening note."

"Yes, he told me that at the library."

"We were sure it was Phoebe, the library assistant." Suzanne joined Maddie at the open serving window.

"So were we – for a time," the detective admitted. "Until our investigation took a new turn in Brian's direction." He wagged a finger at them. "Let the professionals handle it from now on, okay?"

"Yes, sir," Maddie replied, thinking she was speaking the truth.

For now.

The End

I hope you enjoyed reading this mystery. To discover when the next Maddie Goodwell mystery will be released, please sign up to my newsletter at: www.JintyJames.com

Have you read:

Visions and Vanilla Cappuccino – A Coffee Witch Cozy Mystery – Maddie Goodwell 2

Magic and Mocha - A Coffee Witch Cozy Mystery – Maddie Goodwell 3

Enchantments and Espresso - A Coffee Witch Cozy Mystery – Maddie Goodwell 4

Jinty James grew up reading Enid Blyton's Famous Five and Secret Seven mysteries, as well as all the Nancy Drew books. Later on, she graduated to mysteries written by Agatha Christie, Elizabeth Peters, and many other authors. It was her dream to one day write her own cozy mystery, and now she has, with plans for many more.